Ms. Highsmith is a prolific author of contemporary and historical romance, mystery, science fiction, and memoir. Originally from California, Annette attended Yale University and found herself captivated by New England, where she now lives and works.

To Paul, Enni, and Jason. Blue, Green, and Brown.

Annette Highsmith

NEWPORT

AUSTIN MACAULEY PUBLISHERS™

LONDON · CAMBRIDGE · NEW YORK · SHARJAH

Ordering Information
Quantity sales: Special discounts are available on quantity purchases by corporations, associations, and others. For details, contact the publisher at the address below.

Publisher's Cataloging-in-Publication data
Highsmith, Annette
Newport

ISBN 9781645758716(Paperback)
ISBN 9781645758723(Hardback)
ISBN 9781645758730 (ePub e-book)

Library of Congress Control Number: 2020924222

www.austinmacauley.com/us

First Published (2021)
Austin Macauley Publishers LLC
40 Wall Street, 33rd Floor, Suite 3302
New York, NY 10005
USA

mail-usa@austinmacauley.com
+1 (646) 5125767

I'd like to thank friends and family for putting up with my endless scribbling each day, and the hermetic lifestyle that results.

Chapter 1

It isn't your typical day at the SharkFin Tavern. The wind rips through the tangled little streets and pounds at the door, asking to come in. And not very politely.

My hands are chapped and weathered. I can't even believe that they're mine. You'd think I was a fisherman, like so many other folks in Newport, but it wasn't my calling. I suppose the wrinkling comes from years of pulling on the beer tap. And of course, serving hot bowls of chowder. I have the burns to prove it.

Being a bartender wasn't my calling either, I promise you. But it came naturally to me. And I'm a fool for a good story. You hear a lot of great stories behind the bar. One of the greatest of them all began with a lady right across the way.

Annie sits at her usual table, and has that damned computer in front of her face. I hate it when she does that, but it's her 'portable office' as she calls it. I wish my office was portable. I'd take it to Ireland. Always had a thing for that place. It runs in my blood.

She looks up and winks at me, and I flush with a bit of pride. Annie is my girl, and always will be. Not in the

Biblical sense, of course. I just wish she hadn't been through so much.

"Another," she says with a voice that I know means she's stressed. The only woman I've ever seen stressed when she's in a dark, quiet tavern, drinking whiskey on the rocks.

"Soup to go with it?" I ask, filling a glass with ice and reaching for the Jameson.

"I'm okay. Thanks, Tony." She doesn't look up.

I frown a little.

Just because I care for her doesn't mean I have to act like her Jewish mother. But for crying out loud, she doesn't eat enough.

I lift my brow. "Whatever you say."

I fix the whiskey and carry it her way, trying to lean over to see what's on the screen. Something brilliant, I imagine with pride. She's been busting out those books of hers for years now, and from what I'm told, they're selling nicely.

People that know of Annie and come to the SharkFin say they read her stuff on their Kindle. Makes me roll my eyes every time. I just think of a fireplace.

I notice the customary knit in Annie's brow. She's concentrating hard. I would like to talk with her more, but as always, I keep my distance.

Now, let me explain here: Annie ain't young, but she ain't old either. I am. That much is plain.

No, Annie is still beautiful. As beautiful as that fateful day that she came into the SharkFin for the first time. It was as though she were carried in on a gust of wind and snow, not unlike the kind that's blowing outside today.

But I get ahead of myself. That story is yet to come.

Just now, Henry runs through the door and I'm reminded that the story ain't so sad after all.

"Momma!" Henry cries, with June following close behind. That old lady – older than me – sure does take great care of that boy.

"Henry!" Annie shuts her computer, throwing out her arms.

They embrace, and I have to smile. Henry's getting big, and he looks so much like Jack.

Jack is the other piece of this story.

He and Annie were like peanut butter and jelly. Peas and carrots, bread and butter. All that crap.

Trust me, I never believed in this kind of thing either. Not until Annie came to town.

Getting ahead of myself again. Forgive an old man.

"We went sledding," Henry says with joy, throwing his little arms around Annie's neck.

"Well, I didn't go sledding," June says with a hearty laugh. "I can promise you the last time I went sledding was back when we were the 13 colonies." Customary June humor.

Hard as nails, June Clements. I think Annie took a lesson from her.

"Well, we made it in one piece, didn't we, Henry?" June says, clutching her rather large knitting bag. She carries it everywhere. "Annie, I made that pot pie I told you about. It's in the car. I put it in one of those fancy Tupperware deals that has the top that spins in and clicks. About time someone thought of that."

11

"Oh, June. You're the best. Just when I thought I'd have to subject myself to another night of Sloppy Joes." Annie makes a stinky face at Henry.

"I love Sloppy Joes," he replies, doing a little dance with his hands.

The red hair is a dead giveaway that Henry is Jack's kid. And the blue eyes.

"Annie, I don't know why you make that sludge." June collapses into a heavy wooden chair and throws her sewing bag to the side as if she owns the place. "You could afford to order from King's Palace," she adds, gulping a glass of water.

King's Palace is considered 'fancy' Chinese food in Newport. They've got the mystical lobster aquarium to prove it.

"It's Henry's favorite." Annie nuzzles him closer.

"You still on the Tuscany thing?" June asks, leaning her heavy chin into her hand.

"Yes."

By 'Tuscany thing,' she's referring to the novel Annie has been working on for months now. Set in Tuscany. Annie went to an exchange school there after high school.

"Must be nice," June says, twirling her shell necklace between her fingers. "We're in a blizzard and you're writing about Tuscany."

Annie smiles. "You wouldn't believe the things we do to keep sane."

Then she takes a sip of whiskey.

Okay, I gotta explain something here. It's nighttime, it's a Saturday, and it's snowing out. The tavern is empty and

Annie isn't drinking hard. She'll have one, maybe two, then put it away.

Also, there's a Christmas tree in the corner with blinking lights, and she's celebrating an anniversary of sorts.

In fact, it's the first time I've seen her drink whiskey in over a year. But why should I need to explain? We all have our vices. Mine is watching old motorcycle movies and eating peanut brittle. Go figure.

Gave up booze a long time ago. That's why I can tell this story with a modicum of clarity.

All of this is to say that Annie is okay. You don't have to worry for her. Yet still, it's been six years, so I do worry about her on this night.

Six years since she met Jack.

So, now that I've got you interested, let's jump back in time to when it all began.

Annie left New York City in a storm of tears, nearly rivaling the one that was bursting outside her rental car windows. She was 30 at the time. Annie never told me that, but I just ended up doing the math.

She truly didn't know where she was going, but she knew that if she stayed in New York, she'd be 'dead in a year.' Why she would perish in one year's time was unknown, but she said it would be so. And I believed her. Everything Annie says ends up becoming oddly true.

Her heart had been pulled from her chest. Every time I think of it, I still want to punch a hole in that guy's face. She had been in a relationship with some big wig, and at the time, she didn't tell me who it was.

And it didn't matter.

When she took that feverish ride to Newport, she was a young woman who experienced what it's like to have a broken heart for the first time.

I've had my fair share, so I don't think having a broken heart is all that big of an ordeal. But now that I know Annie, I know that the blow was not the normal, garden-variety kind. Annie loved deeply and she loved purely, and nothing had ever gone so wrong before in her life.

"I'll take a whiskey, neat," she said. Her face was chapped red and her eyeliner halfway down her face. She carried a small duffel bag and nothing else. Annie was soaked to the bone, shivering.

Of course, I felt bad for the girl. She wasn't from around here; I could tell that much immediately. We have this joke in Newport that the newcomers stink more than the fishermen.

She collapsed into a chair, which later, when she was in a saner frame of mind, would become 'her' chair. On that night, it was the first one that she could find. Her vision was blurry from the drive, the blizzard, and the tears. She cried the whole way from New York, and she screamed.

I'll never forget that hoarse voice.

"Don't be stingy," Annie said as I approached the table. I looked down at the neat whiskey and it looked like plenty to me. But not one to want to disappoint my only customer, who I was beginning to feel bad for, I walked back to the bar and gave the whiskey a top-off.

When I returned to the table, she managed a little smile, as though apologizing for her conduct. She didn't have to apologize. I had seen worse.

"You looking for something to eat?" I asked, and there began our ongoing joke. Ask Annie if she wants something to eat when you're dying to hear the words 'no thanks.'

"No thanks." Annie cupped the glass in her hands as though it were hot cocoa.

I went back to my post and cleaned up some. Had inventory to do, and mostly I didn't want to butt into the girl's business.

Her behavior wasn't strange, just a little striking. Now, I've seen some interesting behavior at my post, to say the least. But I can say that Annie had that quality you see in an animal after they've had a trauma of some sort.

Her eyes trailed off into the distance, blank and open. She was processing, that much I could see. She was thinking about something, whatever 'it' was. Trying to figure it all out. To solve it. Or perhaps just to convince herself that if she thought about it long and hard enough, maybe it would disappear into thin air, as though it never happened at all.

Polishing the glasses, I looked up occasionally to find her in the same place. Just staring. And sipping.

Now, how it could be that Jack Spencer should come in that very night, I have no idea. He didn't like coming into the tavern. Never did. But he was chilled to the bone and his boat was diverted back from Maine earlier that day, as the storm reports guessed that things were going to get nasty.

"You look surprised," Jack said coldly to me, just as cold as the icicles in his beard. His lips were chapped and blue, that much I could see in the dim light of the SharkFin.

"You mix surprise and happiness." I cleared my throat so as to maintain my rough exterior. Let me admit here that to the outside eye, I did look a bit rough. Even back in those early days.

I won't give you too many specifics, but just imagine the bartender in your local hole-in-wall, and that's what I look like. A little wiry, a mid-size belly. But with a collared shirt on. I like solid colors.

"Happy," Jack huffed sarcastically, dropping his large frame into a bar stool. He didn't have to ask. I knew that Jack only drank beer, so I poured him a Guinness.

"You look tired." I noted that even at the tender age of 35, Jack was sporting some bags below his crystal blue eyes.

Still huffing, still sarcastic. "Thanks."

His beer placed before him, Jack turned his head towards the stranger in the room. Not that he had overt interest, but when there's a lone female in the rooster shack, a man is required to turn his head.

It seemed to me that Jack was detached from what he saw in Annie's bright green eyes, framed by smudged liner. Those eyes were past question dramatic.

And Jack didn't get mixed up in drama.

I always knew that about him. A simple guy. Of the earth. Since he lost his wife, whatever capacity he had for drama, which was nil, shrank even more.

And yet, for a moment, I could perceive that Jack wanted to turn his head again, to look at Annie once more, but he stopped himself.

Annie sat there blinking, also slightly confused by the eye contact she was so briefly engaged in, and returned to her blank state. Jack returned to his fatigue and his beer, and all was settled in the world.

But I'll tell you this, and I don't tell a lie. For a moment, I could have sworn the temperature in the room changed when those two saw each other for the first time.

Chapter 2

"Here comes trouble," I said when I saw the gang piling in through the door. The gang was Jack's fishermen friends. From the look on Jack's face, I could tell that he was hoping to escape from them.

"Never thought I'd find you here," Gregor said, patting Jack on the back. It was a hard, heavy blow. But Jack was a big guy. Stout. He didn't bat an eye.

Rory nodded to me. "Hey, Tony."

"Hey, there," I replied, getting started on Rory's gin neat.

The gang consisted of about three other guys as well, I can recall. But Gregor and Rory were the only blokes I really knew. The former was a Russian import; came into SharkFin from time to time. Rory, however, was Jack's childhood friend.

Similar to Jack's hefty build, Rory was, however, much more compact and poetic in temperament. Was once the 'Hamlet of Newport.' Always walking around with a book. Wanted to write, too. But as it turned out, there was nothing for him in the world but fishing. It was hereditary.

Jack didn't turn his head. "Can't I have a beer in peace?"

"Ain't nothing peaceful about the world today. Your beer time is no exception," Gregor said with mischievous glee. He sat beside Jack and immediately turned his head towards Annie, who was nearly through her whiskey.

Gregor turned back towards me as though I would be able to explain the girl. I couldn't, so I just raised my shoulders in a shrug.

"This storm will make us broke," Gregor said with distain. His dark coloring blended right into my dark-wooded bar.

Jack was dismissive. "I've seen worse."

From the corner, I noted Annie's eyes returning to the men at the bar. Perhaps she was annoyed. Maybe she wanted silence, instead of Gregor's penetrating, albeit light, Russian accent.

But what I at first took to be frustration changed immediately. Annie seemed intrigued. Maybe the tumult and rustle of fishermen was comforting to her.

Despite the initial interest – each man turned his head to Annie one after another – the men went back to their own business. Soon the smell of fish and chips wafted through the air, and the creamy aroma of chowder.

They ate heartily, talked loudly, and drank copiously. Nothing was out of the ordinary.

It was when I saw a few of the men talking conspiratorially and looking in Annie's direction that I knew trouble was headed our way.

Now, these were a few of the guys I didn't know so well, so I wasn't sure what they were capable of. But a particularly tall fellow – let's call him Bill – who I was later told was a new guy on the boat, made his journey over to Annie's table.

He'd had a few beers in him already, so his spirits were high. And his courage.

Bill grinned. "I'm sent on a mission." Annie looked up. Her eyes were dry at that point and she was on her second whiskey.

Sensing the imminent loss of peace, I could see Annie collecting her duffle bag, no doubt to get a head start on settling up her tab.

"Oh?" Annie feigned ignorance. She didn't want to hear about the man's mission.

"See that guy over there?" Bill asked, pointing back to the bar and signaling his friend. "He requests your presence."

Now, Annie has never been one to care if anyone requests her presence or not, but she was also a girl bred with good manners, and so she felt compelled to be polite in the situation.

Annie smiled and looked down at the table. "I'm really just here to have a drink. But thank you."

The smile was the problem. In retrospect, I can see it clearly. It gave the wrong signal to the fisherman, and he persisted.

"Oh, come on, now. Baby, it's cold outside!" Bill said this loudly, so that his friends could hear it. He was proud of his wit.

"I'm alright over here, thank you."

That is when I saw Jack bristle. If I know anything about Jack, it's that he's a gentleman through and through.

Always pained him to see a lady pestered, and I noted that tense muscle in his jaw.

"If I have to carry you over to that bar then I will," Bill said with a laugh. That's when Jack really seemed to lose his patience. He clutched his beer tightly between his large palms.

Annie looked flustered and rifled through her purse, throwing some cash onto the table. I was just about to intervene when Jack did all the talking.

"Come on, man. You're bothering her. Let it go." Jack's voice was measured.

"What am I doing? I'm having a good time!"

Annie got up from the table. "Excuse me."

"Listen, sweetheart, I'm just trying to be nice," Bill said, stopping her by putting his hands on her shoulders, lest he be misunderstood.

That was when the temperature in the room markedly changed. Rory looked petrified, Gregor just laughed, and Jack decidedly stood from his seat.

"What are you doing?" Annie protested, not at all liking the feeling of having Bill's paws on her.

Already in a weak state, I could tell that Annie was holding back tears. On any other day she might have been cool and collected, but it had been a long day.

She looked up into Bill's eyes, and all at once before a tear could form in her already red eyes, Bill completely disappeared from sight.

She'd tell me later that it was a strange thing. One moment he was there, and the next moment he was gone.

What had happened, to everyone's surprise, was that Jack had forcefully grabbed Bill by the back of his weathered plaid shirt and pulled him quickly out of Annie's path.

Before he knew what hit him, Bill was lying on the floor at the feet of a few barstools. And before Annie knew it, the path was clear.

She thought to run out of there quickly, but before she could go, her gaze caught Jack's, for the second time that night.

Something about the look in his eyes gave her pause. His eyes were icy, for sure. Always had been, even when he was a kid. But there was something else there that she saw and couldn't explain. It was pain.

Their locked eyes finally came loose and Annie was out the door. Nearly knocked over my Christmas tree.

It was a short drive to Annie's bed and breakfast, and all the while, peering out into the darkness illuminated by headlights, she thought of the mysterious red-headed guy.

Annie threw down her duffel bag on the Victorian bed and collapsed, staring up at the ceiling. She told me that she just stared for a while, trying to orient herself.

Always strange ending up in a new town when it's dark out. You can't quite tell where you are. Easy for me. I know Newport like I know the back of my hand.

And it sure was pretty at night that time of year. All those twinkly Christmas lights shining in the empty streets.

But I know that Annie felt empty that night in her room at the bed and breakfast. Like she didn't know if she did the right thing.

She had come to Newport years earlier, just for the day. With her mom. Showed me the sweet picture of the two of them splitting a lobster roll by the marina.

So, Annie returned to Newport on a whim. Had fond memories of her brief time here.

But it wouldn't be till the following morning that Annie knew she had made the right decision. It was as though the sun had shed some light on the subject. Annie looked out the window of her room, pushing back the heavy curtains, and saw that blanket of white snow, and the water off in the distance.

Everything looked clean and pure, and just the blank slate she had been searching for.

Annie still wore the same clothes from the night before, and hopped in for a quick shower before going down to breakfast.

To her amazement, she was the only one in the place.

Now, I know Newport Hollows B&B. Been around a long time. And would you believe it, June Clements was the owner. Still is.

When June saw Annie come into the dining room, she started beaming. Someone to feed. And trust me, I know that June prepared a feast.

"Well, good morning!" June cooed. She wore her favorite Newport, RI, t-shirt. It had sailboats on it, and she wore her same shell necklace.

"Good morning." Annie was a little embarrassed that she was the only one there.

Now, we've already discussed how Annie wasn't much of an eater, but on that occasion, June was able to accomplish the unthinkable.

Before she knew what happened, Annie had a large bowl of yogurt in front of her, covered with granola and berries. She was relieved at first, thinking that that was all she would have to face. And the yogurt tasted good; creamy and tart.

But to her dismay, the second course was placed in front of her. June gave her most winning smile.

"Toast and eggs," she said. "They're from my friend Trudy's farm. Fresh as the snow."

"Thank you," Annie said softly. Truth be told, she never liked eggs.

"Oh, and the bacon and waffles are coming out shortly!" June ran back to the kitchen.

Annie tried to protest, but June was too fast and quickly out of sight.

June was real fleet-footed back then. Still has enough speed and energy to chase Henry around, though.

Coming back into the room, June saw Annie covering her eggs in ketchup, and she frowned. Such a shame to drown perfectly good eggs in ketchup.

June continued to talk through the meal, and truth be told, Annie was quite happy to have the distraction.

She was told an earful. Annie learned all about June's book club, garden club, and the Newport Mansion Society, which played dress-up every year around that time.

It wasn't long before June got Annie to agree to wearing some formal 1800s' attire, and gave her orders for a specific Jane Austen book to read for the book club.

Of course, Annie had already read all of them. But she didn't mention that.

It was when June started bringing up eligible bachelors for Annie to meet that she decided it was time to part ways.

Annie got up and excused herself. "If you don't mind, I do have to get started on some work."

Sadly, her laptop was broken at the time. If you ask me, she probably chucked it at the wall when that guy broke her heart. So, she was resolved to check out the local internet cafe to take care of business.

Annie said it was mostly odd jobs then. Writing articles, websites; that sort of thing. She could work remotely, and that meant she could get out of New York and still make ends meet.

June frowned, hating the idea that Annie would have to go out into the cold to that dreaded internet cafe. June never liked that place.

But Annie insisted, and she was out the door.

It is here that I'll change directions a bit. Annie never likes me talking about her old writing days. She tells me it was the unhappiest she's ever been in her life. Writing about all that plain nonsense.

So, instead, I'll tell you about this little gem:

Jack had slept poorly the night before. The wind kept him up, and he was used to waking at 4am to get on the fishing boat.

Since there would still be no fishing that day – the next storm was on the horizon – he decided instead that it was a walk that he needed.

Walking down Main Street, Jack knew that a good strong cup of coffee would amend the fatigue, and perhaps get him through the cold morning. Barringer's Coffee was his supplier of choice, and Jack couldn't help but get the enormous blueberry muffin to go along with it. Pretty much the size of a baby's head, those muffins. But Jack didn't flinch.

Stepping back out into the cold, coffee and muffin in hand, Jack's spirits lifted, until he saw that car driving the wrong way down a one-way street. And they're tight streets there, down by the marina.

He hollered. Always hated when those damn tourists did that kind of thing. But when he saw who was behind the wheel, he couldn't help but smile. And trust me, Jack had never been a smiler.

"Hey!" he cried, waving his free hand in the air, which was still clutching a muffin.

Jack saw Annie's bemused expression in the driver's seat, and finally the look of recognition on her face.

Annie actually had to lean into the steering wheel to look closer, trying to be sure that what she was seeing wasn't an apparition. She knew those icy blue eyes, and that copper hair.

Annie waved her hand to acknowledge him before getting out of there damn fast. Her heart was pounding and she began to blush.

Jack just watched her as she drove off feverishly, and for a moment, it worried him that Annie was driving like a maniac. Perhaps the girl with the smudged liner and the glass of whiskey was just as crazy as she seemed the night before.

Or maybe she was just scared. Running away from something, he thought. Jack was always curious about people's real motives.

He waited till she was out of sight and then continued his journey along the marina. The muffin quickly vanished. So, did the coffee.

Jack watched the boats gently swaying in the breeze; a breeze that would turn into a powerful wind, keeping his sea legs from going where they were inclined.

His heart sank when he thought about it. It always felt like a kind of prison when he was stuck in Newport, of all places. It was the town where he was born and raised, and the town that dished out far too much tragedy for him to even comprehend.

For a fleeting moment, Jack wondered if the winter storms had kept him stuck in Newport for a reason. If the house had kept him stuck there for a reason. Time to face things?

He shook the thought away. Didn't believe in that kind of stuff.

Chapter 3

The day took forever, the tasks were endless, but Annie felt something different, just being in Newport. She sat in the cozy internet cafe with a warm chai at her side and hammered away at the computer, knocking off each item on her list. Every now and then, she gazed out the window and looked at the snow.

The warm glow of the sun reflected off the sheet of white, to the point where it was blinding. But it was beautiful, nonetheless.

Max Caramachi, the owner of the cafe, kept looking Annie's way, curious about the determined out-of-towner. He wanted to make small talk, just like I always do. But he refrained. Sensed the girl was decidedly focused.

Now, if I know anything about Max's cafe – never been there myself – it's that the pastries are damn good. Better than Barringer's. He supplies our cannolis at SharkFin so I have a first-hand experience of what a genius Max is. His family is from Sicily.

All this is to say that Annie didn't eat any pastries, but she did have two chai lattes before the work was complete.

And that was about the time that the storm started brewing. In Newport, it can come out of nowhere. One second you had blue skies, the next second you had a doozy.

So, it came as a shock to Annie when, upon leaving the internet cafe, the heavens turned black.

Annie made her way back to Newport Hollows wearing her heavy purple winter coat, clutching herself.

Getting into her blue rental car, Annie huffed a little. The very thought of when she would return the damn thing filled her with panic. But Annie reminded herself, as she still does, 'one day at a time.'

Annie needed that little saying. She learned it from her mother. It's common enough, that phrase. But looking back on things, Annie says that it got her through hell.

Sounds dramatic, I know. It's a certain kind of hell. Annie sometimes refers to it as 'champagne problems,' when she's trying to write it all off. But it's hard to judge anyone when they're going through hell. Sure, the hell of starving and having no money is different from the hell that Annie was going through. But you can't judge a broken heart, nor can you truly understand it.

This I can most definitely say in regards to Jack.

He spent a lot of time by the water that day, waiting for the storm and thinking about things.

Sometimes I wished that I knew his hell better. I even wished that it was my own, so he didn't have to feel it so much.

Looking back, I think that what was about to happen between Annie and Jack made perfect sense. They were in the same place; like two lost children. Life had dealt them a serving of shit. Pardon my language.

It does to everyone, at some time or another.

But the particular flavor of shit – sorry, again – was the same for them, at that exact time in the world.

They were both heartbroken and lost. They were damn afraid of how they were going to get through it. And very importantly, they both were swimming upstream. Annie, with a smile. Jack, with his rough exterior.

Inside, they were homeless. Outside, they couldn't see that they were being bombarded with love.

Sorry, I'm getting all sentimental. There's a story to tell, and it continued the very next morning.

"Ten days till Christmas!" June exclaimed at the breakfast table, pulling out an advent calendar and handing Annie a little piece of chocolate.

Annie took it and popped it into her mouth. It tasted incredibly sweet and filled her with momentary glee.

"Tell me about yourself." June plopped into a seat near Annie's.

Now, the last thing Annie wanted to do was talk about herself. I know this because nothing has changed. But on that morning Annie opened up, and it would save her, in the end.

"What's to tell?" She was toying with her eggs using her fork.

"I can tell that there's a lot to tell. I've been around a long time." June knew an interesting person when she saw one.

"Well, I came here because I need a little beauty right now. Don't know how long I'll stay."

"Oh, we want you to stay a long time…" June said with assurance. It would give her a chance to hone her matchmaking skills.

Annie laughed. "I don't know where to end up."

"Where are you from?" June asked, resting her chin in her hand, as she is accustomed to doing.

"I'm from Washington. Seattle. Moved to New York to start my writing career. Went to NYU. Things went really well at first, and then they sort of…fizzled out." Annie still played with her eggs.

"It's not your fault," June said, having heard many similar stories.

"But I'm afraid it might be," Annie said, her easy-going exterior becoming indignant. And there were those damn tears again that she was so ashamed of. "I was an intern at a great magazine, I was working on a novel, everything was lining up. I felt really confident. Then somehow it was like things abruptly…started slipping."

"Life has a funny way of telling us to change course," June said with empathy.

"Well, my life told me to get out. Fast."

"You ever married?"

There was a pause as the generational difference sunk in. Annie never wanted to get married in order to support herself. She wanted to be a success. She wanted to take care of herself and not rely on anyone.

Annie didn't even need to explain this to me. I saw it as clear as day. She was left in the funny place of being firm in her convictions, but wondering if she had sacrificed too much.

But Annie wasn't traditional in any sense. Couldn't be. She held firm that she could have both. Love and career. Independence and companionship. It just hadn't worked out yet.

Finally, Annie replied.

"I've never married, no." She smiled, but there was a pained expression there as well. "Wasn't sure whether or not I'd be good company."

At that, June had to laugh.

"I was married three times, and I think my company was very good. It was my husbands' company that I didn't care for!"

The two ladies laughed together. Those girls haven't stopped laughing ever since.

June felt a pang in her chest. She could feel Annie's pain. She knew Annie was going through a lot, and life didn't even get that much easier.

"Oh hell," June said, picking up the advent calendar again. "We're going to jump ahead here." She picked out two extra pieces of chocolate from days 9 and 8.

"What are we going to do tomorrow and the next day?"

"I may need to buy another advent calendar." June paused for a moment and pulled out day 7 as well.

In the hours that followed, Annie's spirits lifted. It was the companionship that perhaps she desperately needed. She and June had a long talk over breakfast, which led to a long afternoon tea, and culminated in an evening glass of wine by the Christmas tree.

They shared stories; Annie about her disillusionment with how she thought things should go, and June reminding her all the while that things turned out okay in the end.

"Don't say 'the end.'" Annie nibbled on June's homemade bruschetta. "That's morbid."

"You're right." June was introspective. "There is a lot more to come. But for now, I must admit that I'm happier in Act 3 than I was in Act 2."

"That's not like a traditional play. Things usually go wrong in Act 3," Annie replied wryly.

"Yes, my play would be very boring."

"I don't believe that for a second."

"It's true. I'm going to be happy in the end. I've decided on it." June took a sip of her wine and gazed at her Christmas tree. It had chili lights on it that she bought in Arizona.

June always said she'd retire in Arizona, but I knew she'd miss the cold weather.

It was right when June was going to move on to more important matters, such as who she would send Annie on a date with, when things got pretty interesting.

That night, Jack Spencer came knocking on the door. Actually, he just burst right in. And he was soaked with water from head to foot.

Chapter 4

The pipe ruptured just before 9pm. Something to do with the frost.

The old house that Jack had been fixing up, known as Leavenworth, was an inherited disaster. That much was clear. Jack learned how to fix up houses as a young fella, before he became a fisherman. So, he knew a big burst when he saw one. Jack wouldn't make it through the night in that house.

So, he did the only thing that he knew how to do; Jack went to June's. He'd been raised around June. I'd seen it happen. June was friends with Jack's mother.

June told him – when she knew he was repairing Leavenworth – that if there was ever a problem, like the one that he had that night, then he shouldn't think twice about coming to Newport Hollows. Jack obliged.

It pained him, really. He'd just as well sleep on the boat. But sometimes, even a man as headstrong as Jack Spencer had to admit defeat.

I'm told that he was quite a sight when he came through that door. Not only was he dripping wet, but a good portion of it had frozen in his hair.

So, it came as a shock to him, literally freezing and angry out of his mind, when he saw Annie sitting there by the tree, drinking a glass of wine and chatting with June. Just earlier that day he'd seen her asking for a car accident.

Annie's first inclination was to say 'Wtf' – she had explained that acronym to me – seeing the cavalier way in which Jack burst into the room. She sprang to her feet, but June remained in her chair, jaw agape.

"Jack…" June finally said, putting down her glass.

It was the first time that Annie had heard his name, and for whatever reason, she thought it was a remarkable name, and well suited.

"Pipe sprung at Leavenworth." Jack spoke flatly, shaking his head.

"Oh, no!" June exclaimed, putting a hand over her mouth. "Did you bring dry clothes?" The mother in her took over.

Jack thought it was the oddest question in the world.

"Afraid not," he replied, thinking he'd just come to Newport Hollows and crash for the night, sorting things out the next day.

"Well, then. I've got some things upstairs." June scurried off quickly. She still had Earl's clothes. Had been some 10 years since he had been gone.

Upon June's departure, there was a penetrating silence in the room. Annie was speechless, and Jack felt a little embarrassed about his predicament.

But I know from both sources, they were mostly happy to see one another.

Jack noted immediately how different Annie looked. The disheveled, frightened lady from the night before had given way to a woman that was cozy, relaxed, and had a look of contentment. There was healthy color in her cheeks.

As for Annie, she saw something very different in Jack as well. His guard was down.

"I'm Jack." He stood in the middle of the room, without defense.

"I'm Annie," she replied, not sure if she should lift her hand to wave in the silly way she'd done that morning. "Is it cold out there?"

Annie most definitely wanted to kick herself. There was no excuse. Especially for someone from New York. But, something about Jack overwhelmed her.

He walked over to a chair and sat, rubbing a spot on his knee where the pipe had ruptured and struck him. There was a bit of blood, but it took Annie a moment to see it.

"Oh no." Annie sprung towards the wound. "Are you alright?"

"This is nothing," Jack said with customary lack of care.

That kid's arm could have been falling off and it would be nothing. Forgive me for calling him a kid, but he was, in my eyes.

"Can I get you something?" Annie thought she could fetch a damp cloth. A band-aid wouldn't cover it.

"I guess a paper towel would do."

Annie jumped up to find a washroom where she could get a paper towel, but in her concern, she thought it was inefficient.

She ran into the kitchen, still smelling of the evening's meal, pasta and bruschetta, and grabbed a white towel.

It seemed like the least practical thing to grab, but it would be more absorbent than a silly paper towel. She soaked it in water in the sink and turned to momentarily glance at a picture of June.

In it, June was standing with a man that Annie assumed was Earl. They were smiling. The setting was tropical, and June looked happy.

Annie came back into the dining room where Jack was then standing, looking at the ornaments on the Christmas tree. He was mesmerized, actually. There was something childlike about it.

"I have this," Annie said, getting down on her knees and wrapping it around Jack's wound.

He looked down to watch the gesture, thinking nothing of it at first, but then it became too overwhelming and he pushed away.

Annie was startled, unsure if she had done something wrong.

"Do you just want to take it?" She handed the cloth over.

"Thank you," Jack said, a little flustered. He took the cloth from her hand and their fingers brushed.

It was a suspended moment. Not unlike the one they'd shared when they first made eye contact.

Jack walked away and sat again in the chair, wrapping the cloth around his wound.

"I need to thank you, for last night."

"It was nothing. That guy was a jerk," Jack replied, still looking down at his leg.

June came into the room carrying an armful of clothes. "I have some stuff here. They should fit. Earl was big around the middle, and you're big around the shoulders. It should balance out."

She stopped, noting the tension in the room. It was that temperature change that I was talking about the night before. She could sense it as well as I could, and it froze her.

At a later date, June would tell me about it. And she would also tell me about a premonition. June was prone to them. Went through a phase of reading palms.

On that particular occasion, her premonition included both something wonderful and something dreadful.

And she saw a baby.

That night, Jack lay in the Blue Suite wearing old Earl's pajamas. It was unsettling to him. He glanced out the window and noted that the storm had passed. The air was calm and still.

There was no caroling off in the distance, as was customary for that time of year in Newport. Jack actually felt relieved by it. That damn caroling always annoyed him.

It was yet another night where Annie and Jack found themselves looking up at the ceiling, waiting for sleep to come. Only that time, Jack was looking up at his ceiling, and he knew Annie was above him.

He knew so little about her, and thought that maybe it wasn't best to learn more. Jack leaned over on his side and tried to let his mind go blank.

Unfortunately for him – I understand this because it's my same affliction – all the most painful thoughts came just at that time, between day's efforts and night's long-awaited sleep. Horrible thoughts. The ones that the business of the day had kept at bay.

Annie, as well, knew that Jack was below her. They said goodnight on the stairwell so she saw what room he went into. She didn't mind that he was down there, but there was a brief moment that she looked down at the floor and knit her brow.

This was when, as Annie recounted to me years later, whiskey in hand, she assumed the only reason she was infatuated by the taciturn fisherman was because she was trying to recover from a broken heart.

Annie doubted her attraction, as any sound-minded woman would. She was on the mend. I guess, you can't even say that. The mending was yet to begin. Her wound was fresh and excruciating. She was still dizzy from it. I remember from the past, when my heart got ripped out of my chest, everything felt heightened. More severe.

Lying there, Annie realized that it was the second night in a row that Jack was strangely on her mind.

In the end, sleep didn't come hard for either of them. The beauty of the silence and the charm of Newport Hollows put their cares to rest, and it wasn't long till they were awakened, not by the sound of alarm clocks, but the smell of blueberry pancakes.

Some guests have remarked that June funnels it through the pipes in order to wake her guests. If she has, I gotta pick her brain. I should be funneling the smell of chowder out onto Main Street.

It was probably 7 am when the smell roused them both.

Jack felt his stomach growl, but Annie wanted to lie in bed all day and just be bathed in the fragrance of it. In the end, her hunger ruled and Annie came downstairs to the dining room.

She was immediately struck by the image of Jack, sitting by the frosty window and devouring a stack of cakes like a hungry animal.

The image was heartening, and Annie couldn't conceal a smile.

Jack, upon seeing her, crumpled to perfection from a good night's rest, cleared his throat.

"I nearly fell out of bed when I smelt it," Annie said, walking over and seating herself at the table beside his.

Jack looked over furtively, seeing that she didn't sit with him. But of course, she wouldn't, he reasoned. They hardly knew one another. Yet still, it seemed like it just wasn't right.

June was standing with a plate of hotcakes before Annie could plop her bottom in the chair.

"Quill and paper," June announced, placing the pancakes before her. It had always been June's way; preparing pancakes in various shapes dependent upon what she knew about each guest.

That morning, Jack got boat-shaped flapjacks.

Annie brought her hands to her cheeks. "Oh, my goodness!"

"They taste just the same as normal cakes," June explained, hoping the shape wouldn't turn her off.

"Better," Jack replied, knowing full-well that June's cakes were the best he'd ever had. And by that time, he had a belly full of them.

"Thank you." Annie picked up her fork and knife. Something about Newport was giving her an appetite.

"Bacon, Jack," June said, by way of a statement and not a question. She rushed back to the kitchen and Annie was left to indulge in her first bite.

"Did you sleep alright?" Jack asked, not knowing why the hell he asked it.

Jack had never been touchy-feely, I must note. Therefore, asking how someone else had slept was foreign to him.

Annie had never slept so well in all her life. "Like the dead." The entire time she'd been in New York City, she hadn't slept a wink.

June presented the bacon. "Well done." She knew that was how Jack liked them.

"Thank you, June. This is a treat," Jack said humbly. Truly, he never ate as well as when he was in June's company.

"I don't know what you poor guys eat out on those boats. Would have made your mother batty to think of it."

For a moment, Jack bristled, and Annie saw it.

Jack dug into his bacon. "It's pretty simple out on the boat, I'm not gonna lie."

"And at Leavenworth. Do you cook?" June asked, immediately regretting it.

Jack went silent. Leavenworth on its own was a touchy subject, but his living there alone was yet another. June shook her head, wishing she could retreat to her room on the basement floor.

"Never have been much of a cook," Jack replied with decency.

"And the work there is…"

"Coming along."

June could tell that he was eager to change the subject.

"And you, Annie. What are you up to today?" June felt as though the room had gotten a little hot.

"Oh, just some work."

"What do you do?" Jack asked far too quickly.

41

"I write."

"What about?" Considering the manner in which she arrived in town, it made perfect sense. But for Jack, there was nothing impressive about it. Only yeoman tasks were impressive.

"Oh, just nonsense," Annie replied, hoping to not talk about it further.

"She wants to write a novel." June was brimming with pride. "We talked about it last night."

Annie spoke far more sheepishly than she should. "I do like to write stories."

Annie could be too bashful; I know that about her now. She never gave herself any credit.

Jack took another bite of his bacon. "What kinds of stories?"

"Well...I don't know." Annie was dreamy, looking about the room. She gazed out at the blanket of white snow just outside the vast Victorian windows. For a moment, the very idea of it made her feel expansive. There were so many possibilities. "I think I might like to write about the sea," she said, her love of Melville overtaking her. "Or Paris," she added guiltily, knowing how inconsistent she was.

Jack smiled. "The sea or Paris."

"I suppose so."

June noted the opportunity and capitalized upon it. "Well, Jack can tell you about the sea. He can take you on the sea!"

Annie turned to him and their eyes met. She thought about how much she desperately wanted to go out on the water. To feel the wind in her hair, and have the sense that she was riding away from things. Off onto a new horizon. She was desperate for it.

Annie looked down at her watch and felt her stomach lurch in her throat. "Oh, I have to go." She rose from her chair.

"Is everything alright?" June asked, not used to people in Newport getting on with such a start.

"Yes, it's just that…I have to start working by 9, or the day is shot." Annie rushed out the door.

Both June and Jack regarded her with wonder.

"She'll slow down a bit," June said hopefully.

Not wanting to make a comment about Annie, lest he might be giving himself away too much, Jack got up from the table.

"I gotta go fix that house."

"And when do you get back on the water?" June asked, knowing full-well that it was where he was most at home.

"Don't know." Jack wiped his brow. He was back in his own clothes, after June had washed and dried them through the night. "Maybe in a week."

"Well, that will finally give you a good chunk of time here in Newport! We haven't had you stay in quite a while."

Were it up to Jack, he'd be gone for years on end.

"Just to work on the house…" Jack said, giving a purpose to his stay. "That's all I'm here for."

Jack walked out into the cold and stood still, bringing his hand to his opposite elbow. For a moment, seeing him through the window, it made June think of John Wayne.

Jack didn't bother to put on his winter coat. He'd just be walking to his truck, and that was that. Back to

43

Leavenworth, where he'd await the plumber and get to work on other things that needed fixing.

His mother let the home fall to shambles when she was alive. But then again, she didn't have anyone to help her in the matter.

I could explain this further, but it might pain me too much.

But I'll mention here that Leavenworth wasn't just a house. It was a mansion. Jack never liked that word.

Chapter 5

Annie stumbled into SharkFin around noon. The moment I saw her I perked up. We had the usual crowd that afternoon; locals that came for a hot meal in the midst of a frigid day. But there was something about Annie that made a room come to life.

"Could I see a menu, please?" she asked, seating herself at the table where she first sat.

My ears perked up like a dog and I grabbed the old plastic-enclosed menu with glee.

"Take your time." I ran back to the bar to grab a Cobb salad that had been placed there, waiting for me to bring it to table.

The Cobb salads were good at SharkFin. Actually, I can honestly say they were the best in New England. It was a local favorite.

But Annie was going traditional that afternoon. She ordered the chowder and I found myself bursting with pride.

She jotted down notes on a yellow notepad, which I later learned was a way to organize her flummoxed brain.

When the soup came out, it was as fragrant and hot as ever. I dare say, it was probably Jack that caught the clams for that soup.

Annie looked at it with wonder and took a big spoonful. A pink flush came to her cheek from the warmth of it, and I poured a refill of beer for Hank, our drunk regular. Hank used to be a fisherman, but then devoted his time to beer and football; a retirement that I envied.

Annie motioned for me to return to the table and I did so dutifully, although I admit, it was never my desire to serve folks food. It was something I only engaged in with the afternoon crowd. But when it came to Annie, I would have served her up all of Newport on a platter.

Annie looked mischievous. "Can I ask you something?"

"Of course," I replied, never one for words. Except the words in this story, which I take pride in.

"Do you know that guy? The one who protected me?" I could tell that she was embarrassed that she was even asking. She shouldn't have been, because it was an important question.

"I know him well." I spoke casually, not trying to give away how much I knew the kid. Okay, he's not a kid. I have to get that out of my head. "He lives in Newport on and off. Been here while fixing up a house." I immediately regretted it. It sounded too familiar, my statement. Like I knew all about Leavenworth. Which I actually did.

I was called away to replenish a basket of bread and was momentarily glad about it. I didn't know how much more I could explain to Annie.

Small town life seems quaint and without consequence, but I've learned that when you dig up one shovel-full, you're getting into a whole mess of things.

Once served, Annie sat quietly with her meal, and for some time I saw her staring at the flashing Christmas tree

46

near the entrance, with that same vacant look that I saw the first night she came to Newport. She was dreaming of something, I didn't know what.

I walked back over, hoping I might replenish her soup or give her something else.

"You see the town yet?" I asked.

Let me note now that this was out of character for me. I've always been fond of where I live, but never proud. Never directing tourists towards the next showy thing. But I sincerely wanted Annie to see the sights. I wanted her to love Newport. Oddly, I wanted her to stay.

"Not much, no." Annie looked around a little apprehensively. She was a strong woman, no doubt, but still had reservations about dining alone.

"You need to see the mansions. Especially this time of year." I picked up her empty plate, all the soup gone.

"I hear they're beautiful."

"They've got this dress-up occasion."

"The costume thing."

"Yes, that's it," I replied, liking the light in her eyes.

"June was telling me about that."

That's when I first learned where it was that Annie was staying, and who was her host.

I liked her a lot on first sight, but I liked Annie even more when I learned how much she liked June. Good people like good people.

"You're staying at Newport Hollows?"

"I am. It's wonderful," she replied.

"How long you staying for?" I realized that I was still awkwardly holding her empty soup bowl in my hands.

"I don't know." Again she was looking off with that distant stare.

"Well, we'll have you as long as you want to be here."

Annie looked up at me as if no one had ever said such a thing to her before. Funny that that should be.

"Thanks. That's nice to hear." Her thoughts turned inward. "I'm sorry, but is that man –"

"Jack," I said quickly, filling in the blanks.

"Jack. Is he…alright?"

"In what way?" I asked, not understanding her meaning.

"I don't know, he just seems so," she paused for a moment and cleared her throat. "Sad."

That was the lone word that she could think of. There was a sadness to him. It was clear as day.

But what Annie didn't know – and what I did know – was that she could see it so clearly because she felt it herself.

I tried to keep my response as general as possible. "He has seen a thing or two."

"Well, he seems very nice," Annie finally said, getting a hold of herself. "I'm grateful for what he did the other night."

"I'm sure it was his pleasure."

I made the statement clear enough. I saw what was going to happen. But Annie was too hard on herself back then to see when something good looked her in the face.

That very same day, Annie sat in the Newport Book Club, held at the Newport Public Library, wondering what had happened to her life.

Sure, she was happier in the wee few days since she had come to Newport, and yet, she had ended up in a public library with women twice her age, talking about Jane Austen.

It was all too formulaic.

Still, she couldn't help but feel comforted by it. Talks of Mr. Darcy and Elinor and Marianne were far more enjoyable than life itself.

Listen, I have not read these books and I don't know these characters. My wife loved them, though.

A sort of calm came over her as she sat in that stately room, with years of history. The Newport Library is historic, I must add. She felt a certain weight in her being released. There was nothing else to do that afternoon but sit, and hear about Jane Austen.

"But don't you think it's sad how all the women had to rely upon men?" Myrtle asked.

Myrtle was a curmudgeon, and I must say, is no longer with us. Thanks for the memories, Myrtle. But she always spoke the truth, and shot from the hip.

"That was just society at the time. This still exists," Peggy argued back.

Now, Peggy is still with us, and was married to a rich financier in Newport. She spent her girlhood touring mansions, and finally she lived in one.

June rolled her eyes and spoke under her breath. "We know it still exists." Peggy had come into money by marriage, and June was both repulsed and envious. Myrtle was no less pleased with poor Peggy.

June also didn't approve of Peggy because she was a vegetarian.

"I'm just saying that, it's romantic and all, but their lives were just about marriage," Myrtle went on, noting June's snide comment.

Annie chimed in. "Well, the Regency period was when women started to have a choice about their partners. It was when romance was possible. A woman could choose based upon what her heart told her."

The ladies turned to her. There were about a dozen of them, and the mood in the room lightened up a bit.

Myrtle frowned. "I don't know that I believe in romance anymore."

"Then why are you reading Jane Austen?" June asked with a huff.

"Because there was nothing else to do on a Tuesday night. My husband is driving me crazy. All he does is watch baseball."

Annie spoke and the attention turned towards her again. "I would still like to believe in romance."

Cucumber sandwiches were being passed around. And strangely, Oreo cookies. It was Myrtle's night to bring the refreshments. Clearly, not June's.

A rather large woman named Gayle asked, "Do you have a partner?" Her eyes lit up with hope.

Annie became sheepish and recoiled.

"I'm just sort of…getting out of something," Annie replied, wondering why the hell she should be so embarrassed about not being in a relationship.

There was silence, which June broke with a conversation about her latest knitting project, and the Christmas gala at the Montgomery, one of the larger mansions in Newport.

The ladies discussed their costumes, the food that would be provided via potluck, and the number of guests that would most likely attend.

There was also discussion of the dancing, the live four-piece orchestra, and the traditional reading of the 12 Days of Christmas.

All the while, Annie was kicking herself. Why should it be so damn uncomfortable to tell other women that you're single? It was baffling to her.

More discussion of Jane Austen ensued and Annie found herself thinking about Jack. She knew that she shouldn't do it, but it was something that popped into the forefront of her mind out of nowhere.

Had been for at least three days.

Just like Jack.

He simultaneously was at Leavenworth, sitting in front of a big fire. I can say that it was a big fire because from what I remember of that sitting room, the fireplace was nearly as tall as Jack.

He sat in front of it drinking a beer. Jack stared at the massive flames and counted the days until he could again be at sea.

The plumbers finally arrived that day, fixed the break, then left. That was a relief for Jack, because he was more comfortable at the house by himself. Didn't like to rely on anyone and couldn't stand those ruffly curtains at Newport Hollows. But there was one thing that he missed.

Now, Jack hadn't been romantic with a lady in some time. It's hard for me to say this with certainty, but I know that after Lily was gone, he kept his distance. Couldn't stand the idea of being hurt like that again.

So, it was strange for him to have his mind fixated on a lady. It was something that was only allowed to his former self.

But Annie did capture his imagination. Same way she did mine.

Sitting in the corner of that room, so old and tarnished that one could never imagine that it was once a wealthy estate, there was a Christmas tree. I couldn't believe it when he told me.

Jack was never festive in any way. But something that afternoon inspired him to go down to the lot right on Main Street – run by the Newport Boy Scouts – and buy a mid-size fir. He even planned to decorate it. Went to the hardware store and bought lights. But as he sat there looking at it, the remains of his beer drawing towards room temperature, he couldn't manage to do it. Decorating a Christmas tree alone seemed far too ridiculous.

So, he just stared at it.

Let me boast about the Christmas tree at the SharkFin. I did it myself. All blue lights, flickering in the darkness of the maritime tavern. I even went down to the local drugstore and bought ornaments that were made of glass and glitter. My favorite was a large shiny orb that had a boat painted on it. Made me think of Jack.

And I didn't feel lonely when I decorated it. I never feel lonely at SharkFin. There're always people coming in. And I've been using many of the same decorations for years. It's comforting in a way.

Jack used to love decorating the tree as a kid. But here I'm being sentimental and giving too much away.

What you're probably hoping for now is to hear about when Jack and Annie meet again, and its coming soon. I promise you.

It happened just the following night, a Sunday, when Annie had become addicted to my chowder – alright, it was when she became addicted to my whiskey because she never liked to drink alone – and Annie found herself at my altar.

She was sipping her drink, sitting at her table, when Jack came in to my great surprise and delight. Rory was with him.

Jack's friend was eager to talk about the good ole' days. When they were in school, playing soccer, and gorging on pizza. Jack wasn't as eager to talk about those things, so he listened silently. He was always a good listener.

The two friends went to the bar and Jack spotted Annie immediately. Consequently, he had trouble focusing on what Rory was saying.

Annie had the same reaction. It was like everything became heightened. She didn't know if she should ignore him or get up to say hello. Did they even know each other? Were they close enough yet to acknowledge one another?

Jack nodded his head towards her. Again, it was his John Wayne temperament. Annie nodded back, but added a smile.

Rory continued to talk, ordering his gin, which I supplied before he said a word.

But it was Rory who was the first one to make a scene about Annie's presence.

Rory's voice was hushed. "There's that woman again."

"Yeah," Jack replied without feeling.

"She's good looking."

"Sure." Jack knew full-well that when one man showed interest, it piqued the interest of the others.

He didn't want to peak Rory's interest.

"Remember the other night when you –" Rory began to say.

Jack cut him off. "Just drink your drink." The event was only days ago, and Jack didn't want to think that his barroom scuffle was anything other than just a thing of the past.

"I would go talk to her, but I'm afraid that I'd end up on the floor." Rory took a sip of his gin.

Jack just shook his head.

I watched this little interaction and brought the guys a plate of mozzarella sticks. They didn't ask for it, but I provided it gratis. I was just thankful that the recent storms had kept them on terra firma for so many days.

"Thanks," Jack said, giving me a cutting glare. Now, Jack always had that look, I must say. But for me, I'd been on the receiving end of it for many years. I was used to it.

"Eat up," I replied, returning to a bit of chopping and zesting.

It's embarrassing to say that a large part of my job was chopping and zesting, but so it went. My days were filled with lemons, limes, and oranges.

It was around that time that a gentle snow began to fall. I could see it outside my porthole. And by saying that I have a porthole, I'm being literal. There was a porthole behind the bar, and from it, I could see the harbor just a few paces away.

I went to the radio and turned on Christmas music. I'm nostalgic, so help me. Christmas was a week away. What can I say?

Josephine, the old lady in the kitchen – older than me – who had been working there since God-knows-how-long had been baking bread pudding, and the smell was wafting through the joint.

The combination of aroma, Annie sitting there, and Jack sitting there, just went to my head.

I ran into the kitchen to get a fresh plate of the pudding. Josephine scolded me and said that it was too soon to serve it. But I figured it was never too soon to serve dessert.

I took a huge pile and put it on a plate, carried it out of the kitchen, and walked towards Annie's table. I placed it before her ceremoniously.

Her eyebrows lifted. She was as intoxicated by the smell as I was. Yet she was intimidated.

"Is that for me?"

"It is." There was a boyish grin on my face.

She picked up her fork with wonder, then shook her head.

"I can't do it alone." Annie looked towards Jack and felt his eyes on her. "Do you want to help?"

Jack smiled softly.

"I'll help you!" Rory said with enthusiasm, rising from his barstool. Jack knit his brow, seeing that his friend was swooping in.

Annie laughed to herself, and delighted in seeing Rory sit across from her, ready to indulge. He asked me for another fork and I ran back to the bar. Jack looked tense.

I brought Rory a fork, and he quickly took a large portion of the pudding. Placing it in his mouth, he moaned with glee.

Annie was surprised that he dove in with such relish. But she was about to see him dive in even further. Rory was quick to interrogate her.

"I've seen you here before," he said between mouthfuls.

"Yes, I'm starting to like this place." In the corner of her eye she could see Jack, regretting that he hadn't come to join them as well.

"How much more do you want? Because I could eat this whole thing." Rory noted that Annie had only had a spoonful.

Annie put her fork down. "Just dig in." She tried not to look at Jack again, but she couldn't help it.

Rory went to town on the dessert and finally Annie spoke up. She couldn't help herself.

"Do you want some?" she asked, directing her voice towards Jack.

Jack smiled at her, then looked away. He was beginning to be incensed by all the smiling she brought out of him.

"I'm good, thanks," he replied curtly.

"Suit yourself."

From a distance, Jack watched her bringing fork to mouth, placing the pudding in her mouth and chewing. It shouldn't have been erotic. It was a normal act of being human. But there was something totally remarkable about it for him.

Jack smiled to himself and shook his head. He was losing his wits. Clearly.

"You still at the Newport Hollows?" Jack finally called out.

"Yes, still there." Annie toyed with the fork in her hand. She wanted to say more. She was even thinking of staying in Newport for quite a while.

Annie had never stayed in one place for too long. But she was beginning to wonder if she might take a chance on this town.

I couldn't have worked it out more perfectly myself.

"How is the wound?" Annie asked.

"All patched up."

"And the house?"

"Not patched up."

Meanwhile, Rory watched the distant exchange and wasn't happy about it. He kept glancing back and forth, from Annie to Jack.

Rory decided to dive in. He began some light conversation with Annie that rolled into introductions, talk of hobbies, and the weather.

"Have you ever been sailing?" Rory asked. Jack heard it and stared into his beer.

"No, actually, I...haven't."

"We should go."

I saw that knot in Jack's jaw again. He wanted to intervene. Jack was good at intervening. But the past prevented it.

Jack and Rory were always immensely competitive. Like brothers. And in that situation, Rory seemed to have the upper hand.

Chapter 6

The exact moment that Annie felt the sea breeze in her hair, Jack took a hammer to an old wall.

It was two days later, and Annie and Rory had agreed upon the right time when they might go for a sail. It was fair weather outside, and it was only a hitch in his boat that was keeping Jack on the ground. One thing after another prevented him from leaving Newport. Perhaps the biggest thing was that he still hadn't asked Annie out on a date.

She was becoming a town regular, and quickly. Jack saw her almost daily; at the coffee shop, the pharmacy, the SharkFin. She just kept popping up.

Knowing that it was the day she was out on the water with Rory, Jack decided it high time that he tore down a wall at the mansion. It just felt good. And he was mad at himself, not Rory.

Jack hadn't felt inclined to ask a woman out for many years. Annie was the first to make it seem like a pressing issue, but Jack didn't give in to the desire. He sunk himself down in contemplation.

Lily, God rest her precious self, had even told Jack that when she was gone – she knew she was going – she wanted him to find someone else. Didn't trust Jack to be alone. He couldn't cook or clean. Wasn't even keen on buying new clothes.

Jack would absolutely not listen to Lily when she told him that. The agony of it was too great.

I do remember that, during Lily's decline, those were the years where Jack's beard grew, his shirts became holey, and his diet was comprised of Hungry Man frozen meals. I kid you not.

Even though he avoided the SharkFin during Lily's tough months – said he didn't want to see that look in my eye – every time he made a rare appearance, I'd fill that guy with about as much food as I could find. In the back, Josephine would put more butter in the chowder, put more oil on his meat, add cheese to his fries.

Now, there wasn't a need to fatten Jack up. He's always been a well-built guy. But during that time, he was getting a tad sinewy. Even Hungry Man meals weren't enough for a furnace like Jack Spencer.

I digress, but my point is, Jack wanted to spend time alone with the mysterious Annie from the Big City, and was even given permission by the late missus, but still, he couldn't do it.

And because of his cowardice, that very afternoon his old friend was enjoying her company. And a double blow: they were out on the water.

Jack gave that wall a serious beating.

In fact, he probably got a week's worth of work done in that one afternoon, running around that old manor like a madman.

He became motivated to finish the renovations quickly, sell the damn thing, and finally move to Maine. Maybe

Vermont. Hell, anywhere but Newport. With all its money, history, and tourists, it was not the best fit for someone like Jack.

He could live in a shack by the marina and be perfectly comfortable, so long as he got up in the morning and got right on his boat.

But there were family ties that Jack had to attend to. Demons that he couldn't escape. And his internal demolition on that mansion was just another way of killing those demons.

Jack stopped and felt the sweat trickling down his brow. Even though it was cold as hell in that old house, the sheer exertion of Jack's efforts brought a sheen there.

He was wearing a white tank top in the middle of winter for crying out loud. But I already mentioned that he was a human furnace.

So, Jack looked out the window. Out towards the sea. Leavenworth was on a steep hillside, so he could see the water clearly. Everything was grey; the sky, the sea, the hillside.

Christmas lights were twinkling in the town, of course. And the big tree on Main Street was in view.

For a moment, it softened him, and Jack thought again about decorating his own tree.

Maybe it was okay to be alone, to be heartbroken, to be lost, and still to open yourself to pleasure in life.

That moment was fleeting, because then Jack spotted a lone boat out on the water.

He knew that it was Rory's.

They were in the cabin because it was cold as sin. Annie was bundled up in her purple coat, and Rory looked quite at ease behind the captain's wheel. It was a small vessel; not a fishing boat. Just a ship that Rory used to ride as a kid. His cheeks were pink from the cold.

"Do you need more coffee?" Rory asked with a smile, seeing Annie clutching herself. He had brought a little portable pot.

"Oh, that would be great." Annie watched as Rory poured another serving into a Styrofoam cup.

"Is it everything you hoped it would be?" Rory asked, his finger gracing hers as he handed her the cup.

"You mean, being on a boat?"

"No, I was referring to the Maxwell coffee," he replied humorously.

Annie laughed. There was something smart and intelligent about Rory that she liked. She considered if maybe they were there on that boat together for a reason.

"It is amazing." She looked out towards the grey sea. "I just can't imagine living like you guys live."

Rory felt defeated for a moment. He didn't want to be roped in with all the other fishermen. He didn't want it to be his identity. Especially considering the treatment that Annie received the first night that she came to Newport.

I'll say this much about Rory. He was a good-looking kid. Always had a way with the ladies. But he found himself entering into his 30s without a wife, wondering what the hell he had done wrong.

In Annie's eyes, he saw potential. I just know it. Someone vulnerable, looking for a safe haven. I don't want to say that he saw his children in Annie's eyes because that kind of stuff turns my stomach. But Rory had some definite intentions.

"My father was a fisherman, and I was determined to do something else. I wanted to be a writer," he said with pride.

"Oh?" In truth, she couldn't imagine why the devil he would want to do that.

"Yes, I wanted to write the next Lord of the Rings. And then I realized that I just wanted to read Lord of the Rings."

Annie had to laugh again. She thought about how interesting it was; what we're motivated to do with our lives.

"What do you do?" Rory asked, liking that he was making her laugh.

"I'm a writer."

Rory's eyes went wide, and his grin even wider.

He was thinking that the prospect of starting a romantic relationship with Annie was becoming even more alluring. If just to live vicariously.

"I promise you, I don't write anything interesting. Just boring stuff." Annie took a sip of her coffee.

"Have you written any stories?" Rory asked, trying to incrementally draw himself closer to her.

"I tried to write this book set in Paris. I visited it briefly, years ago. It's been on my mind ever since. I got halfway through writing it, then I just stopped. It was like fight or flight took over. I couldn't go back to it."

"You got halfway through it and stopped?"

"Yeah, I think it was a good story, too. About a woman down on her luck who moves to Paris to study art. Changes her life, etc. I guess it sounds a bit formulaic."

"No, that sounds nice."

"I've actually never told anyone that I got halfway through that book," Annie said with an embarrassed smile. "I was just so upset that I froze up like that."

"There's still time. You're not dead yet." Rory placed a finger under her chin.

It was an intimate gesture, and Rory knew that he had done it too fast. He pulled his hand away and turned back out towards the sea.

After a good half hour of chatter and tepid coffee, Annie got too cold and Rory's confidence was flailing. The weather report wasn't good that day, but Rory hoped that Poseidon would be on their side anyhow.

The grey had become heavier, darker, more ominous. Rory knew instantly by the look of it that the storm was returning. It had been a particularly violent winter.

"I hate to say this, but I think we'd better go." Rory turned the boat around.

Annie was relieved. "Will you be spending time with Jack tonight?" She asked a bit too impulsively. She's always been impulsive.

Rory looked at her quizzically, wondering if all that time his hopes were unfounded.

"No, Jack keeps to himself." Rory was annoyed yet again that Jack stole the spotlight. He tensed his jaw and continued to spin the boat 180°.

"Yes, I think that Tony told me that."

Rory gave a nervous grin. He knew a hell of a lot more about me than Annie did at that time.

"Tony," he said dismissively.

"I like him," Annie protested. This is not for sure, but I choose to write it here.

"Jack's been working on the house, mostly. Well, at least trying to. Feels guilty about it."

Annie turned to him. "Why does he feel guilty?"

"Because of all that money." Rory spoke casually, still looking out to sea. Rory tried to explain. "He'd just as well get rid of it all. But Jack feels the weight of that history. That legacy."

Annie had a confused expression on her face.

She didn't have a clue what he was talking about. Why was Rory speaking in hushed tones? Hell, why do I still speak in hushed tones about it?

Money had been in Newport since Newport was Newport. And I can say – I haven't seen all of Newport's history, even though it feels like it – Jack Spencer might have been the first to consider Newport wealth as a curse.

"Isn't there some other family member that can help with the burden?" Annie asked.

Rory paused and chose his words.

"Tony wouldn't be able to do it. The family disowned him a long time ago."

Annie was confused. "You mean, SharkFin Tony?"

"Jack's father."

Annie didn't ask anything more, feeling as though she had stumbled upon a landmine.

Our story is a kind of Newport landmine. I wanted to wait before you knew. I'm still afraid that as the story goes on, you're going to begin to see my character as a villain.

But I can't get too serious at this juncture. We got a ways to go, and I know that you don't want to hear a sad tale. Too many sad stories in the world, so I'm determined to uplift you with this one, if only a little bit.

64

I hadn't heard about Annie going on that boat with Rory until later that night, when she came into the SharkFin with a cold red nose, shivering. Annie would tell me that she still couldn't get the chill out of her bones from earlier that morning.

"It's crowded tonight," Annie said, sidling up to the bar. We had a nice coat rack near the front door – built it with my own two hands a couple years back – but Annie wasn't ready to take off that purple puffer. Reminded me of a wearable sleeping bag, that jacket. When you combined that with the grey wool hat with a little fuzzy ball on top, and the maroon scarf that looked like it was about to choke her, I had to suppress a laugh just looking at Annie.

"The weather has cleared up a bit. Makes Newport folk come out of their caves," I said humorously, wiping my hands with a damp bar cloth. I turned to look out my little porthole, and sure enough, the skies were clear, but a crystalline frost clung to the edges of the glass.

"It is beautiful out." Annie rifled through her bag to take out a pad of paper.

"You writing me a poem?" I poured her a whiskey without asking if she wanted it. We'd already developed a kind of rapport, and it filled this old man's heart immensely.

Her tone was mock-defensive. "No, Tony. I'm doing work." So, she wanted me to leave her alone? No chance of that.

As I placed the neat whiskey in front of her, Annie reached out and grabbed it with her gloved hand.

"You're a real Newporter now," I said, watching her as she sipped. The booze immediately warmed her cheeks. "You already know the name of the bartender."

"Does that classify me as a Newporter?"

"Sure does."

"Rory told me. On the boat this morning. I can't believe I didn't ask sooner."

I was silent for a moment. That's pretty uncharacteristic of me, but I had to wonder just how much Rory told Annie on that occasion. Of course, I'd later find out that she knew more about me than I wanted her to, but that's life, isn't it? You can't hide your secrets for long. They always seem to come to the surface, like a dead body that you tried to drown in the ocean. Sorry for the terrible image.

"Seems to me like Jack will be able to get back on his boat soon." Annie took another sip and rummaged through her bag yet again. She pulled out a smooth blue pen.

"Well, not so sure about that." I picked up a glass and polished it with my damp towel. "He's a bit conflicted about it."

I was instantly puffed up with pride that she chose to mention Jack in my presence. That was the second time she brought him up in a conversation. I couldn't have orchestrated it better myself.

"Why is he conflicted?"

"Well, you see, he's gotta lot of work to do in Newport. He's been holding off for a long time. Seems like he's intent on sticking around for a while." I tried to be as casually suggestive as possible, suspecting at the time that Leavenworth, and the weather, weren't the only reasons that Jack wasn't getting back on that boat.

"Interesting."

Okay, so I knew that she found it far more than interesting, but that was pure Annie behavior. She was never one to give away too much, but I found that with time she loosened up the reigns a bit. You'll soon see why.

"What you working on there?" I watched as Annie scribbled away, and in cursive. Maybe she did that so I couldn't read what she was writing. You ever tried to read cursive upside-down?

"Oh, just some ideas. For a book."

"Book about what?" I asked, noticing that there were folks at the end of the bar that were trying to get my attention. I ignored them.

"It takes place in Paris. It's about a woman that changes her life."

"Like that Eat, Pray, Love thing? June was explaining it to me." I immediately regretted it. Annie darted a glance my way that could cut glass. "Okay, not like the Eat, Pray, Love, thing," I said, backtracking. Hey, can you blame a guy? The silly book came out the year before. Had a whole crowd of book club members that came into the SharkFin, clutching their copies, ordering plates full of pasta. I couldn't help but think about it. But Annie didn't look pleased by the comparison.

"It's different than that."

"How so?" I wanted to know what Annie had in mind for it. Basically, I just wanted to better understand her funny mind.

"Well, the heroine leaves and never comes back. She becomes a French woman. She doesn't return to her former life."

"Is that what you want to do?" There was a little silence after that as Annie considered my question. Maybe I was pressing too hard, but she seemed like such an open person – *is* an open person – so I knew that I'd get an answer.

"Sometimes. I think about it a lot," Annie said dreamily, sipping her whiskey again. "Mostly, um…" her thoughts faltered as she seemed unsure what to say next. I was clinging to her every word. "I was seeing this guy. This man," Annie went on, and I felt as though Pandora's box was about to open. Made me happy. I wished to pry open that damn box with my bare hands. "I was seeing him when I was in New York. We talked about going there."

"Mm hm." I knew where the story was going. I had heard the likes of it over and over again at my post. "Well, we just recently…parted ways."

At the time, it finally explained the runny eyeliner and empty gaze that I saw less than a week before.

"We always talked about Paris. About going there." Annie circled the rim of her glass with her fingertips. "And he's there now."

Okay, so I gotta say something here. I was confused at first when Annie told this to me, but the fact of the matter was that the guy, the bigwig whom I want to feed to the lobsters, had broken up with Annie and flown to Paris the next day. The place that they dreamed of. Talk about a douchebag, and I don't use that term lightly.

"Why you still want to write about it?" Surely, if that prick tainted the place with his presence, then Annie should dream of somewhere else. The conversation was too heated for me to mention Ireland.

"I don't know. As a kind of escape?" Annie said. I could tell that she was becoming emotional 'cause her eyes were getting misty, as ladies' eyes tend to do in these situations.

"I've finished half of it." It was the second time that day that she let the cat out of the bag.

"You can make it brilliant. I just know it," I said warmly.

"Thanks, Tony. I think I probably could, too."

And that was Annie for you. For all the time she spent doubting herself or being contrary, deep down, she knew that she could do it. She knew that she had all the strength that was necessary. Her mortal flaw was that she needed reminding of it, and often. Hell, I would take that on as a personal job, if she had let me. I wanted to ply her with whiskey and chowder and tell her how great she was, on a daily basis. But young ladies can't listen to old guys. They listen to young guys, if they trust them. And sometimes, even when they don't. Crying shame, if you ask me.

"I gotta premonition for you." I leaned into the bar and rested on my elbows. Nearly killed me, my elbows were so damned knotty. "While you're here, you're going to find all the inspiration you need for that story." It was the kind of premonition June would make.

"You think?" Annie looked down at her notes.

"Yeah, I do think. You wanna know why?"

"Sure."

"Because remarkable stuff happens in this town. Amazing stories. Something may just happen to you, too. Something that will make you feel…like yourself again."

Now, okay. I was assuming that Annie didn't feel like herself since that horrible heartbreak back in New York, but with time, I'd come to discover that it was true. I'd also discover that my premonition had been spot on.

Chapter 7

A couple of days later, June was having a Christmas Luau. Now, before you get all up in arms and blame me for making up such a thing, I'll have you know that that was an annual event. June experienced her first Luau in Hawaii when her husband was still alive, and the dinosaurs, and since then she'd been obsessed. One night while drinking a Kahlua coffee at the SharkFin, she admitted to me that she liked all those Polynesian guys with their shirts off. And the roast pig.

So, it was a time-honored Newport tradition and naturally, since Annie was still staying at Newport Hollows, she was invited. You couldn't hold the thing outside, of course, 'cause it was damn cold, so June hosted the Luau in the drawing room of the B&B. I call it the 'drawing room' 'cause it sounds fancy and whatnot.

I always got invited but never went. Didn't like all that booze around me. That may make you scratch your head, but I felt safe around the booze in the SharkFin. I'm the controller of it. Not when I'm at someone's party, though. I don't feel like explaining more.

Anyway, on that occasion, June pulled an old grass skirt out of the basement and convinced Annie that she should wear it. Don't ask me how.

Annie held the skirt up to her waist. "This is ridiculous."

"Oh, if I had that figure, I wouldn't even bother to wear the skirt at all," June said cheekily.

She did have a fine figure in her day, June Clements. But alas, all of us get old in our own way. June's way was to spread horizontally. Mine was to grow a forest of nose hair.

"I'm not going to be the only one wearing this, am I?"

"Oh, no," June insisted. "The whole book club wears one."

And June wasn't kidding, either. Although she chose to wear her favorite Luau t-shirt, the one that had a picture of a palm tree wrapped in Christmas lights, the other members of the club did as they were told and wore their grass skirts. Some of those old biddies even wore coconut shell bras over their sweaters. You see why I didn't want to go?

Although everything about the book club made Annie feel ridiculous, she had to admit that a big smile came to her face whenever she was with those ladies. They embraced her and took her in like a pack of ferocious den mothers. Looking back on things, Annie needed those den mothers.

Peggy was not only dressed in Luau attire, she was also sporting a diamond tennis bracelet, black pearls from Tahiti, and sapphire earrings.

"Is this a luau or a Sotheby's auction?" June asked, full of disgust.

"I feel like a mermaid," Peggy replied defensively.

"You look like an ancient shipwreck."

71

The smell of poi and roast pig filled the air, as did the aroma of sizzling Spam. I'm not going to say anything more about that one.

Annie clutched a glass full of Pineapple Extravaganza, June's version of a boozy, island cocktail. There were so many different kinds of liquor in that thing that myself and every other bartender on earth would have cringed. But it tasted so sweet that none of the dames knew it had so much liquor in it. Good thing June had already arranged for a horse-drawn sled to take everyone home.

June approached Annie, delighted by the warm smile on her face. "You having fun, honey?" June had a plate of festive finger food in hand.

"It's nice." Annie moved the mini umbrella aside in order to sip from her straw. "Everyone seems to be having a good time."

"I invited Jack, but I don't think it's his scene," June explained with a sigh. Annie seemed to choke on her drink when June said that. Apparently, she was caught off guard.

Annie stifled a laugh. "No, I can't imagine him here."

"Oh, I see." She saw the blush on Annie's cheek. "You just imagined him wearing a grass skirt, didn't you?"

"No. I just mean that…he doesn't seem like the luau type."

"I don't know," June went on, grasping Annie's arm and holding it tight. She was always grabbing onto people like that. "I think that you might like to see Jack Spencer dance with fire!"

"Oh, stop it!"

"Ain't no one in Newport who hasn't dreamt of seeing that," June added, nudging Annie in the side.

As the Luau continued, Annie found that the Pineapple Extravaganza was going to her head a little. That, coupled with the fact that June always kept the B&B at a cozy 80°, explained why, after the massive buffet and coconut macadamia chocolate cake, Annie felt like she needed a bit of fresh air.

She walked outside and felt the brisk wind on her face. Hey, I wasn't there but I'm just embellishing. Annie took a deep breath and then felt her phone buzz in her pocket. She hadn't received many messages since coming to Newport, and she wasn't sad about it either. Newport brought some peace back into her life, as I knew that it would.

But when she looked down, Annie found perhaps the last thing that she wished to see. Or maybe the first thing. I guess it depends on how you look at it.

It was from the bigwig. The celebrity. He'd sent her a picture from Paris. Annie would tell me later that she went right up to her room after that. Didn't even say goodbye to anyone before she did so.

The following morning, Annie still couldn't rip that picture from her mind. Not only did the guy tear her heart out, he then squeezed lemon on the wound. She couldn't figure out whether or not he did it intentionally, but knowing how Annie liked to always think the best of people, I assumed that he didn't realize what he did. How it made her feel.

Waking up the next morning, Annie could smell the pancakes. At the Luau the night before, June made a big show of boasting how there were going to be pineapple coconut flapjacks. Despite Annie's enthusiasm, she found that the next day she didn't have the stomach for them.

She told me later about how she needed to go to the shore that morning, to feel the wind in her hair and breathe in the salty breeze, but it was some years before Annie told me what happened next.

It's funny when I look back on it, because I saw her as she walked down Main Street, heading to the path that took adventurers and wanderers along the water, past some of the most impressive mansions in Newport. You wouldn't believe how many tourists you found on that path during the summer. But during the winter, the only person you'd find crazy enough was heartbroken Annie.

As I was saying, I was coming out of Barringer's coffee at the time. I desperately needed a cup of Joe in order to receive the huge shipment coming in that morning, enough seafood to feed all of Santa's elves. And to be perfectly honest, I also needed a fresh apple fritter. It was hot, right out of the oven, and my cardiologist would have killed me.

So, I was walking along, happy as a clam with my morning bounty, and then I saw Annie drifting along. I didn't stop to call out to her because there was something about her expression – looking down towards the ground, hands in the pockets of her purple coat – which gave me pause. She was a hell of a lot heavier in spirit than she had been days before, and you know, I didn't want to intrude.

Annie finds her way to the path – which she learned about from a brochure in the Newport Hollows lobby – and she looked out towards the water, thinking about things, I suppose.

Was she feeling pain? Regret that she never responded to the bastard that sent the Paris photo? Or even worse, was she contemplating what she might say to him at any

74

moment, with some lingering hope that they still had a chance?

All that really pisses me off, so I ain't going to go into it much further, but let's just say that Annie had a lot on her mind.

Now, when Annie is feeling low about something, she can't write. That's the clearest sign that I have that something is wrong. She won't touch the laptop, she won't check emails, and she barely even looks at her phone. Annie always told me it's because she can't concentrate, you know.

I never have that problem. When life deals me lemons, I squeeze them into a cocktail at the SharkFin and my cares are dissolved.

Now, as Annie was walking along – in my opinion, desperately searching for some reason to feel happy, or relieved – she looked up at those beautiful Newport mansions on the cliffside and something did lighten within her. You gotta understand how beautiful these places are around the holidays. Imagine if Marie Antoinette had a Christmas party at Versailles, then you'll understand.

Those great stately mansions, as old as dirt, but still looking like new, were wrapped up like Christmas presents, head to toe in fabrics and ribbon, tinsel and expensive holiday lights that you can't find at the drugstore, but only at, say, Williams Sonoma, and Annie found that she could smile again. In the misty, silver sky of morning, those mansions were like beacons of color and light and hope. It sounds corny but I'm not making this stuff up. It's the Newport Christmas effect. It's legendary. Just ask Google.

Annie was walking along with a new spring in her step. The mixture of briny air, moisture on her skin, mansions dripping in opulence and good cheer like the North Pole had barfed all over them; all of that came together and filled Annie with some hope. Hope that she'd get through this thing. She'd get over the douche on holiday in Paris. She'd start a new life. Finish her book. See the world. Everything that I was of the opinion she deserved, in that moment.

What caught her attention, aside from the gorgeous lighthouse on the other side of the water – more of that to come – was a particularly run-down mansion on the very edge of the cliff, where the channel met the sea and sailors found that they were beginning their journey to the unknown. There, on the edge, was the one mansion with not a lick of holiday embellishment. It sat sadly on the edge, looking out towards the grey, tempestuous horizon, its antique green paint peeling from the pressure of wind and sleet.

There was a single light on inside the house, on the bottom floor. Annie had to wonder if it was really possible that anyone lived there, and also, how it was that they let the house go to seed.

She kept going down the path, curiosity drawing her towards that house like a petite blonde drawn towards a cabin in the woods in a horror movie. Okay, it's not that bleak, but it was just an analogy.

Annie kept walking, finding that she was getting closer and closer.

Of course, I could've told her who lived there. Anyone in Newport could. But it still amazes me that she was drawn to Leavenworth on that blustery morning.

Chapter 8

As Annie got closer, she saw someone standing in that front room; the one with the light on. The windows pointed out towards the sea, framed inside them was a hulking man with reddish hair.

If you don't already know at this point that it was Jack then you're way behind on the story.

So, seeing Jack, Annie's jaw dropped open and she just stood there, staring at him. You know, I can't blame her, 'cause he was a good-looking kid. Always was. Got it from his dad.

That was another joke to make sure that you were paying attention.

So, just when things couldn't get more surprising, Jack, standing in that window, thinking of God-knows-what but I bet it was Annie, looked down towards the path and spotted her. Their eyes met. Just like the first time in the SharkFin, the temperature outside seemed to change. Within Leavenworth, the air became warm, and down on the path, Annie felt the same heatwave.

Now, Annie could have been gingerly about it. She could have waved, or simply smiled, but to my dismay she hopped behind a bush. She admitted this to me after the fact, and only with whiskey in hand.

She dropped down behind that bush and Jack knit his brow in confusion, as he often did. But you know what happened next? He chuckled to himself. Although Annie was strange and remarkable to him at the time, he also found her endearing. So, he laughed. He needed that laugh.

Now Annie, still shielded by the bush, realized her mistake and slowly crept out from behind it. I mean, she knew she wasn't trespassing or anything. She wasn't following him. It was all just an innocent mistake, and she was ready to own up to it.

When she came out from behind the bush, Annie looked back up at Leavenworth and noticed that Jack wasn't standing there anymore. Knowing her, she panicked, sure that he probably thought she was pathetic and went about his business.

But Jack surprised her just then by showing up on the path. He came downstairs and out of the house to greet her, not even wearing a coat.

"Are you okay?" Jack asked.

"What do you mean?" Annie tried to hide how mortified she was.

"It's just that, I saw you fall behind that bush," Jack said, pointing towards it.

"Oh, that?" Annie looked back. "I…didn't fall behind it. I jumped behind it."

Annie admitted the truth, and then she covered the smile that crept up on her face.

"I know. I was just teasing you," Jack said. "It was a good jump, though. Do you have a history of military service?"

"I'm afraid that I would single-handedly destroy the U.S. military."

The two of them smiled at one another. And they were both in awe, I know that much. It was the first time they were really humorous around each other, and it seemed to break the tension, as that sort of thing always does.

Jack led the way. "Come inside so you can get warm."

He didn't really wait for a reply, or an excuse, but said it as a fact. He wasn't going to let Annie walk any further in that cold, and he wanted nothing more than to have her between Leavenworth's four walls, even if the place was kind of a dump in progress.

And Annie didn't refuse, because she wanted to spend time with Jack as much as he wanted to spend time with her.

You think I'm sugar-coating this, don't you? Nope. It's all the truth.

So, Jack opened the door and let Annie in, and I gotta explain something here; that place was not as half-bad as Jack made it out to be. In fact, Annie found it to be kind of dreamy. Later, when she explored the fancier mansions, she'd always talk about how Leavenworth had the most charm and character.

That was still before she knew about its history.

But I digress. Annie was flooded with warmth upon entering the place, and Jack walked her from empty room to empty room, sharing what plans he had for this wall and that, that ceiling and the other. Annie heard everything he was saying. In fact, he had her attention fully. But she couldn't help but be a little rattled by his presence.

I know how ladies feel about men fixing things and whatnot, but that was a whole other level for her. Jack was a master with that kind of stuff, and he never wanted any help, so when he gave her a tour of that huge place, describing how he was going to fix it all with his bare hands, she swooned. At least, my lady friends lead me to believe that that is the effect.

Finally, making their way into the main hall with large windows overlooking the ocean, Jack pointed to his undecorated tree and gave a sheepish smile. Amidst the dust, broken walls, cracked stone stairs, and dangling chandeliers, the pristine green tree stood out as a beacon of hope. It was something new, something alive amidst a wreck of opulent history. It was fresh. You could smell the pine needles.

"You should decorate it," Annie said, her good nature always shining through.

"I got too much else on my plate." Jack ran his hand through his hair. He wasn't trying to be vain. Jack was never a vain man.

"I should bring the book club by. They'd love to do it for you."

Jack didn't respond with words, but cringed a little. In truth, he wanted no one but Annie to decorate it with him, probably while sharing a bottle of wine and then dishing up a Hungry Man lasagna.

And for Annie's part, she wished the same as well, minus the lasagna. But it was still too soon. Neither of them could understand the strange sensations they felt around one another.

Jack offered her tea, and Annie had to decline, for the mere reason that she had another meeting. We're not talking AA.

If the Newport Public Library was festive on the previous occasion, it had seriously taken it up a notch on the second. Hell, it was two days until Christmas, and June oversaw the manic decorations herself, so you know they were spirited.

We're talking animatronic Santas, light-up deer that looked like they'd been struck by lightning, and even one of those inflatable Christmas trees that had a whirlwind of snow blowing around inside. It was hard to concentrate on books with all that insane holiday cheer assaulting the senses.

"Do you like?" June asked, throwing her arms out with a flourish.

"It looks amazing in here, June. How do you do it?"

"Do what?" June asked, dangling her shell necklace in one hand and a Christmas cookie in the other. She wore a sweatshirt on that evening that read 'Mrs. Clause' in puffy glitter paint.

"Host all these events before Christmas. First the Luau, and now this. You must be exhausted."

That being said, Annie always admired people who put so much effort into things like that. She never had the mind for it. If anyone wore a festive holiday sweater, no matter what holiday, Annie was in awe.

"I live for this," June replied honestly.

"I think it's wonderful."

"And I have a surprise for you." June ran to the side table and took a box out from beneath it. Of course, Annie thought that she got a present, but it was the kind of present she wasn't expecting. Taking the lid off the box, June handed Annie Tupperware full of pancakes.

Annie recognized the smell. "Wait a second."

"Pineapple coconut. You know I was heartbroken when you missed it this morning."

"Oh, June. I was having a bad morning."

"It's okay honey. Just be sure to eat those while we discuss Jane Eyre tonight. I'm going to be like Joan Crawford in Mommy Dearest until you do."

And so, the ladies gathered in their usual spots, their chairs set in a circle. Everyone wore their best red and green ensembles, and iced cookies and homemade caramels were passed around in even more Tupperware.

"Jane Eyre," June said ominously and reverently, holding up a paperback copy. "One of the greatest books ever written."

"Oh, come on," Myrtle protested, shaking her head. "Yet another story about a woman at the beck and call of a man."

Peggy chimed in defensively. "But they fall in love. It's romantic."

June naturally wanted to mention how Peggy was at the beck and call of a man as well, but she held her tongue. Please understand what considerable force it took for June to do that.

Myrtle had a sour look on her face. "Jane has no other prospects. Of course, she falls in love with him. When you're stranded on a desert isle and all you have are coconuts, you eat coconuts."

That comment reminded Annie that she had a Tupperware full of cold pancakes sitting on her lap, and she began to eat. She didn't wish to see June's Joan Crawford side.

"These caramels are divine," Gayle said, stuffing them in her mouth. It was Gayle's way of dealing with tension; God bless her.

A rather serious girl wearing horn-rimmed glasses spoke. "I do not think that Jane's behavior is built upon need, but rather mutual affection." The girl, Samantha, was a new addition to the book club and seemed intellectual way beyond her years.

"You make a good point, Samantha," June said to the serious adolescent. "Would you like a cookie?" She held out a plate.

"I'm afraid not. I don't consume milk or dairy," the sober Samantha replied.

Although the tense young lady made Annie more than a little uncomfortable, she liked where her mind was going. If Samantha would do the talking, then Annie could focus on getting those pancakes down in a timely manner. They were still good, even though cold.

"Mutual affection, my foot," Myrtle went on. She picked up a glowing, fiberoptic Santa hat that sat on a table to her right and placed it upon her grey head, like she was protecting her mind from nonsense. "The girl had no other choice."

Annie couldn't hold it in anymore. Even with a mouthful of pancakes, she needed to say her piece. She put her hand in front of her mouth so no little bits of Hawaiian pancake came flying out.

"Pardon me," she said, still chewing. The group waited for her to finish. "I think the story is about the quest to be loved. Jane is searching, not for romantic love, but for acceptance. She wants to belong." The group leaned in as Annie explained further. "June, can I see that for a second?"

"Sure, honey," June replied, passing it over.

Annie opened it, knowing exactly which page to turn to.

"If you recall, the passage where Jane talks to Helen Burns, she says," Annie began to read it aloud, "to gain some real affection from you, or Miss Temple, or any other whom I truly love, I would willingly submit to have the bone of my arm broken, or to let a bull toss me, or to stand behind a kicking horse, and let it dash its hoof at my chest."

The women were silent, willing Annie to speak more, so she went on.

"Throughout the book, Jane seeks to gain love, without scarifying herself in the process. She wants autonomy, and also acceptance at the same time."

Annie stopped and looked down at the book in deep thought. Something struck her that she never realized before; she related to Jane Eyre.

"Jane refuses Rochester's proposal for marriage because then she would render herself a mistress, and therefore, she would sacrifice her own integrity. She is presented with a loveless marriage; one that would allow her the meaningful purpose that she craves. Yet still, she is torn between love and integrity."

Silence.

Now, I know that explanation was impressive. I was told that the precocious Samantha even started a round of applause.

But I know that Annie didn't feel any gratification. You wanna know why? She was thinking of Jack, at Leavenworth, and she wondered if he was fond of her in the way that she was fond of him, if only from a distance; or from behind a bush.

Chapter 9

Christmas is a magical time in Newport, and the moment when it hits its zenith, just when you think nothing can be more glorious, it's on Christmas Eve when the mansions of Newport open their doors and lunatics like June Clements dress up as Victorian era imbeciles.

Listen, I don't mean to be harsh. But any kind of dressing up just gets to me. I like the kids that come to trick-or-treat at the SharkFin on Halloween, but I'm talking about the little kids, not the teenagers and drunk adults.

Anyways, June had a whole warehouse full of costumes that she kept pristine throughout the year, so that when the Newport Christmas Gala took place, she was prepared. That meant that she had a dress that fit Annie perfectly, even though Annie secretly prayed that it wasn't going to happen.

Now, I gotta admit to something. Even though I never stepped foot inside a Newport party, the Christmas Gala at the Montgomery was a different story. I was the bartender – cash bar – which was always placed in the 'Grand Foyer,' as June called it. Of course, I pronounced it 'foyer' and June pronounced it 'foy-yay.' So highfalutin.

So, I was standing there and really getting into the cheer of things. I wouldn't wear no costume, mind you, but I had on a red Santa hat and my finest green polo shirt. I cleaned up nicely, if you ask me.

I was pouring eggnog like it was going out of style for the ladies that didn't want to look like they were conspicuously drinking, and then I poured double shots of scotch for their husbands. The ones whose wives made them dress up in Victorian attire? I poured them triples.

Everything was going fine and dandy, the Newport High School choir sang carols in the corner, women walked to and fro with those puffy muff things in their hands, and in steps Annie, looking like a vision.

She was embarrassed to no end – that much I could see from the flush on her cheek – but she was radiant. Her costume gown was a forest green sort of color, whereas my green shirt verged more on pastel. Annie looked around the room like she was the most uncomfortable lady on the planet. It always happened to someone at their first Gala. It could be a bit overwhelming, seeing all that pageantry.

Finally, Annie caught my eye and I burst with pride. She walked my way and I poured her a whiskey neat.

Annie fanned herself. "I'm sweating."

"You're wearing a lot of fabric," I replied, pushing the drink towards her.

"It is beautiful." Annie looked up at the ornate ceiling, the half dozen Christmas trees dripping in tinsel, ribbon, and glass ornaments, as well as the 'Bird of Paradise' fountain at the center of the hall, giving it an atrium-like feel. Usually the fountain was illuminated by a vibrant blue light in its basin, but on that night, its colors shifted from red to green, and back again, in hallucinogenic slow motion. I actually had a flashback to the sixties. Those were good times.

"It's the only time of year where Newporters take over this town," I said with pride, leaning against the makeshift bar. "Then the tourists come it, and we cater to their needs."

"Can you imagine living in a place like this?" Annie looked up at the ceiling yet again. The voices in the foyer reverberated throughout the high walls reaching towards the sky.

"Nah, too much space," I said, sipping from my soda water with lime that I had stored near my post. "I like coziness."

"You live nearby?"

"Just up on the hillside there. Got a nice view of the water. But it's cozy enough. I call it a cottage, but Jack calls it a shack."

"I see."

You know, I didn't know at the time that she knew about Jack and me. But I saw that glimmer in her eye, as though she wanted to say more but couldn't, and that was my first hint that she knew something.

"Jack certainly doesn't live in a shack." Annie spoke humorously. I assumed that she was referring to Leavenworth.

"Some call it a shack compared to the Montgomery."

"It has so much potential though."

"You've been there, I take it?"

It was as clear as day. Of course, she had been there. Alone. With Jack. I could sense it in my bones.

"I happened to wander by there and...yes, I went inside."

"And you liked it?"

88

"It was unique. There was something about it that…really struck me."

I wanted to tell her that it was the presence of Jack that really struck her, but I'd never go so far. Not in those early days.

And so, I watched as Annie downed her whiskey, chatted with new friends, and with strangers, all the while smiling, sizing things up, getting comfortable.

It was clear as day to me. Annie was trying to figure out if this could be the setting for her new life. Or at least, the next chapter of it. Not the Montgomery, but Newport.

****

Christmas morning greeted us with a delicate blanket of snow. As Annie awoke in her room, she turned her head and watched it fall. Just trust me on this. But she couldn't lie in the cozy bed for long, wrapped up in her bedding burrito, held in by a floral quilt which June's grandma, Floxy, made by hand. Floxy deserves a whole book of her own but we're not going to go there.

So, Annie was looking out the window, smelling strawberry and cream-topped waffles coming through the floorboards, and for the first time in a long time, she was sincerely happy. We're not talking relieved happy, but fully and truly happy, as she should have been all the time.

Coming down to the dining room, Annie felt no shame in wearing her PJ's. In fact, June had instructed her to do so. The Christmas tree was glowing, invited guests sat around at tables, smiling and enjoying their waffles with eggs, sausage, bacon; the full spread. Annie knew that she'd need to call her folks later, that they'd be pissed that she wasn't home in Seattle, but there was plenty of time for that. In the meantime, she'd celebrate with her temporary family and feel no shame. Annie told me once that she felt a lot of guilt and shame growing up in Washington.

"Bloody Mary," June said, placing it before Annie after she was seated.

Annie scoffed. "June, you gotta be kidding."

"It's Christmas morning. This is serious business, there's no time for kidding."

Annie leaned over and took a sip from her Bloody, complete with a green plastic straw. There was an umbrella in it, which she assumed was left over from the Luau. It was savory, spicy, and utterly delicious, and she couldn't help but taste bacon.

"Bacon-infused bourbon." June winked.

"Jesus."

"Don't take the Lord's name in vain," Myrtle said from a nearby table.

"Sorry."

Annie dug into her waffle and eggs, surprised at the appetite that called deep from within. I suppose being happy gives someone a good appetite.

After a good deal of feasting, Annie looked around the room and made the decision: Newport was the place for her.

You may not believe me, but I felt that moment when it happened. I was sitting on my couch looking at the TV yule log, drinking hot cider. My breakfast was a simple affair; eggs, bacon, and an English muffin with butter. God help me, I'm a simple guy.

But all of Newport shook when Annie came to the realization that she was home. Hell, my cottage shook. I saw the walls move. Or maybe that was just from the sugar in the cider.

Just as a delighted smile came to Annie's face, June approached once again, shiny package in hand. The paper was red and iridescent and the green bow had glitter on it.

"What's this?" Annie asked.

"It's a Christmas present. You're not allowed to turn it down." June took a seat at the other side of Annie's little table.

"June, you shouldn't have."

"Oh, stop being cliché and open it."

Annie tore it open. She always had a thing for presents. Inside the paper was a pretty white box with a lid on it. She opened the lid and set it on the table, peering inside the box. There seemed to be a great deal of tissue paper and nothing else, but Annie tore through all that until she found a silver key. She held it up to inspect it.

Annie knit her brow. "What's it for?"

"It's a key to Newport Hollows. You always have a place here, whether you run out of money or not," June said with a warm smile.

"This is too much."

"It's not too much. I own the place. I can do what I like."

Annie clutched the key to her heart, feeling the tears coming.

"Don't cry." June handed Annie a napkin. "You bring something special to Newport. It's important that you know that."

Annie got up from her seat and came around the table to give June a big hug. They held each other for some time.

June could say some strange crap in my opinion – pardon me – but that was one of the truest things that she'd ever said. Annie did bring something into town that was lacking. I could never place my finger on it. And clearly, I wasn't the only one that thought so.

Jack made his entrance just then. And I know that you'd like it to be on a gust of wind and snow, his cape billowing, his skin blistered from a long journey through the hillside on his horse. But I'm sorry, it's not that kind of story.

Yet still, Jack did make an appearance and he was wearing a blue hoodie. It matched his eyes. He carried a humble package as he looked around the room in a daze. It was Annie's eyes that he spotted first, and it pleased him.

"June," he said, wanting to make it clear that he didn't make his way to Newport Hollows in his truck only to see Annie. Although in truth, I think that was why.

"Jack! We have cannolis." June ran back to the kitchen. He tried to stop her, considering that he had already eaten, but he was too late. Standing with a package in his hand, Jack turned to look down at Annie. "Merry Christmas."

"Merry Christmas."

"I got something for June. Just a little thing," Jack said. "To thank her for the other day."

"She got me a key." Annie still held it in her hand.

"Key to what?"

"Newport Hollows. I guess she wants me to stay. She may regret it," Annie said with a self-deprecating smile.

"I don't think she will."

The seriousness of his voice took Annie off guard, and were she not mistaken, she might think that Jack believed the same.

"Four cannolis," June proclaimed, setting them across from Annie.

Jack laughed. "June, I can't eat four cannolis."

"You better, or you'll hurt my feelings."

"I'm telling you," Jack said, seating himself in a chair and shaking his head. He wasn't resigning himself to the imminent food coma. "I gotta be at the SharkFin dinner later. It's an early dinner."

"Then better eat fast." June, hand on hip, was not taking no for an answer.

"Dinner at the SharkFin?" Annie asked, remembering when I had told her about it.

"It's Tony's favorite night of the year. You should come." Jack tentatively ate a cannoli.

"Do I need an invitation?"

I could have strangled her. Of course, she didn't need an invitation.

"No." Jack met her eyes. "You'll be my date."

Chapter 10

My moment of truth had come. No, not the truth about my deep, dark past, but the truth about my Christmas dinner. Everything lay in the balance, as far as I was concerned. The ham had to be juicy, the mashed potatoes had to be creamy, the green beans had to be crispy, and the chowder had to be hot. Damn hot. I was breaking out into a cold sweat.

But I was happy, that much was sure. It was my favorite night of the year, and only those closest to me were invited. Josephine worked her tail off in the kitchen, and every few minutes I ran back there to make sure everything was on schedule. She bristled every time, and then shooed me away. I didn't mean to pester her.

Not only was the meal smelling delicious from where I stood at my post, but the decorations were done just right. My blue Christmas tree twinkled and glowed, casting a mesmerizing aqua hue across the SharkFin. I also had little mermaid lights that I had found at the Newport Thrift Company the day before, and I dangled those across the bar. There was mistletoe hanging from the ceiling at strategic locations so that guests could steal a kiss. Christmas music played in the background. I favored Judy Garland.

And so, the SharkFin looked its most magical, I was feeling pretty damn sparkly myself, and I was positively aglow when I saw Annie walk in that door with Jack by her side.

"Table for two, Tony," Jack said.

Let me just say here 'cause I know you want me to explain. Jack didn't call me dad. Hadn't since my drinking days. I think I gave up that privilege.

"Coming right up. Wait here."

I inspected the full dining room. Hank had usurped a table for two. Luckily, he was already on his bread pudding, so I decided to take the plate from in front of him.

"What ya' doin'?" Hank protested, already well into his cups.

"You're being relocated," I said in no uncertain terms.

"But I haven't finished my pudding."

"Eat it at the bar and I'll throw in a Scotch."

Hank didn't reply with words but with action. I handed him his plate and he walked over to the bar, no questions asked.

I quickly cleaned off the table with my handy bar towel, got some clean silverware, and the table was as good as new. When I pulled out the chair for Annie, Jack scowled at me. I think that he wanted to do that.

Annie took a seat. "Thanks, Tony."

That night, she wore a tasteful maroon dress. You could see her graceful collarbones. That's all I'm going to say from my end. I know that Jack was delighted, but still curt with me. "You got menus?"

"Have I got menus?" Didn't the kid know where he took the lady? "We got ham, potatoes, green beans, stuffing, and cranberry sauce," I said matter-of-factly.

"Fine. We'll have that."

Annoyance aside, I was determined to serve those two the meal of their lives. I ran back to the kitchen – I'm not kidding, I literally ran – and began to gesticulate to Josephine wildly.

"We got important guests on Table 2. I need magic, Josephine."

"Who is it? The Pope?"

"Don't get smart with me. It's Jack. With a special lady. I need that food hot." I raced out of the kitchen.

Josephine muttered as I pushed open the two-way doors. "I'm too old for this."

Now, while I was panicking and rushing, Jack and Annie sat there peacefully. She looked around at the place in wonder, loving the blue motif – not making this up – and she smiled warmly. Jack was pleased by it, that much was sure.

Before I knew it, I had two hot plates in hand as I came back out to the table. There was a candle lit between Jack and Annie, and it illuminated their two marvelous faces. The image made this old guy very happy to see.

"Madame," I said, placing a plate before Annie. "Monsieur." I placed the other in front of Jack. I tried to be all highfalutin and French, but Jack gave me an embarrassed look.

"Thanks," Jack said.

Annie leaned over her plate. "This looks amazing."

So, I disappeared. Actually, I went back to the bar where I could watch them eat every bite, and also attend to the Christmas boozers that were clamoring for more liquid.

I got busy. Real busy. But every time I looked back at that table, my heart soared.

"This is so good." Annie took another fork-full of mashed potatoes.

Jack spoke plainly. "He does a good job."

I'm glad the kid finally admitted to it. You wouldn't believe the silence I'd received when I made him Mac and Cheese from scratch as a kid.

Jack put down his fork. "I'm glad you came tonight."

"Me too," Annie replied, her cheeks gently flushing.

Now, I don't want to get too touchy-feely here, but Annie was filled with warmth and comfort. What's more, she felt safe. It was a contented feeling that surprised her. But she was beginning to see the pattern every time that she and Jack spent a small sliver of time together. He warmed her to life. That was something that she feared she'd lost the capacity for.

The feelings within Jack were of the same variety, but there was complication, as well. It was the first time he'd had that warm, tingly feeling since Lily was still around. He'd need to wrap his head around that, in a way that only a man could; slowly.

The smell of the bread pudding wafted from the kitchen and straight to my nose. I'd been tasting it all night to make sure that it was continually up to snuff. I had a belly full of it, but still I yearned for more. And I don't use the word 'yearned' lightly. It was just about time to bring two heaping plates to Table 2. In fact, I was on my way back to the swinging doors when I was rudely interrupted by Santa.

"Ho, ho, ho!" Donald bellowed, spreading his arms out wide with a flourish as he entered the SharkFin. Donald was a beloved auto mechanic on Cove St., and every year he delighted in his duty to dress up as Santa. There were a number of other old timers in Newport that could have taken on the task, but Donald just happened to have the biggest belly. "Merry Christmas!"

Everyone took out their phones and I cringed. I could never understand the whole taking-pictures-on-phones thing. I used to do it with a Polaroid camera. Those were the good ole' days.

So, the phone lights were flashing brighter than my poor, overshadowed Christmas tree, and everyone started hollering and clapping.

Donald walked from table to table, taking pictures with folks and stealing food off their plates. Again, I'm not telling a lie, he was notorious for doing this.

"Do you want a photo?" Jack asked.

Annie was bashful. "No, I think I'll be fine without one."

"Come on, it'll be fun." Jack motioned over to Donald. The big guy in red approached the table and Annie covered her face with her hands.

"And what would you like for Christmas, little lady?" Donald asked, getting down on one knee.

"Hold on, get closer." Jack held his camera up to take a picture. He was holding an actual CAMERA. That's another reason why I knew Jack was the only one worthy of her.

Annie and Donald leaned in, and Jack captured the perfect shot. I still have a copy of it on my fridge.

Annie knit her brow. "I don't know what I want for Christmas."

"You're just afraid to say it," Jack said, egging her on.

"Okay, well..." Annie looked down and thought about it. "I suppose I want a place of my own. A place to live."

Donald put a hand on his belly. "Where is that, so that Santa doesn't find you real estate on the North Pole."

Silence followed, and if Jack could've learned in and whispered in her ear, he would have, but to do so would be out of character for him.

Annie smiled. "Well, Newport." Looking at that smile, I think that Jack was transformed. I'm telling you, something that was broken in him came back together again.

Donald lifted his finger and pointed it at her. "You've got it. But only if you've been nice this year, and not naughty."

"I've been nice. Maybe a little too nice," Annie replied, her voice trailing off.

She didn't need to say more. At least I got the gist of it. Being as nice as she was got her into a lot of trouble. I wish she had walked around with armor on, a helmet, or at least a Hazmat suit. It was the kind of protection that she needed back in those early days, when she didn't know how to look after herself.

Donald was satisfied and continued his rounds, eventually finding himself at the bar drinking Bourbon. In his defense, the SharkFin was the last spot on his route so the guy deserved a drink.

That being done, I started my excited walk back to the double doors, intent on finally bringing out that bread pudding, maybe two glasses of port, followed by Irish coffees. I suppose it was vicarious drinking. But, yet again I was thwarted, and at just the same spot where I was stopped dead in my tracks the last time.

That time it was Rory that entered. And for some reason, I knew that he was up to no good.

Rory, dressed in a festive Christmas sweater – not ugly Christmas sweater, but tasteful – spotted Annie instantly and made his way over to their table, pulling up a chair for himself.

Rory sat. "I knew I'd find you guys here."

Now, it seemed brash for him to do so, but you have to understand that Jack was one of his best mates, or at least he thought so, and therefore his treachery was expertly disguised. He was a man with a mission.

"Rory. You just missed dinner. I'm sure you could still get a plate," Annie said warmly, then looked across at Jack for corroboration. Unfortunately, Jack was stone-faced.

Rory nodded his head. "Hey, Jack."

"Hey."

And so, Rory usurped the evening. I brought out three plates of pudding instead of two, and three ports. I can't say that it was unpleasant, 'cause the three of them shut the place down. But it was mostly a conversation driven by Rory, wherein he asked Annie more questions about her writing, how he wanted to get coffee soon to pick her brain even more, and also how he'd like another shot with her out on the water.

Jack stayed silent. He had to. You wouldn't believe the history between those two boys.

Chapter 11

The following morning when Annie came down to the dining room at Newport Hollows, she didn't smell pancakes, she didn't smell bacon, and she didn't even smell coffee. What she found was June Clements lying on the floor, looking up at the ceiling.

"June!" she cried, thinking that something was terribly wrong. She rushed to where June was situated on the carpet.

"Take me, God."

"What's wrong?" Annie feared that she might need to call the paramedics.

June whispered. "Food coma."

"From breakfast?"

"No, from dinner last night."

By way of explanation, Christmas night was the one night of the year that June kept to herself. She didn't entertain, she didn't cook, and certainly didn't go anywhere. June famously ate leftovers and looked at the Christmas tree, thinking of her dead husband. Naturally, you can see why she might have overdone it in the food department.

Annie stifled a smile. "Are you going to be okay?"

"I always recover from Christmas night by New Years," June said, pulling herself up to a seated position with a wail and a moan. "I ate a whole tin of peanut brittle."

"Can I make you some tea?"

"Even that might make me burst."

June sat for a while and did some breathing exercises while Annie rubbed her back. Oddly, Annie found that she had quite the appetite that morning, and so she offered to take June to Barringer's Coffee.

"You'll need a crane," June said.

"Come on. A little movement will be good for you."

So, the two ladies got in Annie's blue rental car and off they went towards Main Street. The sun was shining majestically, reflecting off the harbor and filling all of Newport with the most transfixing golden light. Annie smiled to herself, thinking of the evening before, and the quality time that she had spent with Jack. But there was something still troubling her.

"Do Jack and Rory not always get along?" Annie asked, finally driving down Main Street in the proper direction. She was getting a handle on things.

"It's a long story. I'll tell you all about it when I have a cappuccino in front of me."

"Fair enough."

Walking into Barringer's, the smell of fresh coffee was like a pleasant assault to the senses. Annie closed her eyes and breathed it in. There was nothing like that smell first thing in the morning, and Barringer's had some of the best coffee in New England.

"One coffee, a blueberry muffin, and a cappuccino," Annie said to the petite girl behind the counter.

"Better make it a blended mocha. With whipped cream," June said.

The girl repeated their order. "Okay, that's one coffee, a blueberry muffin, and a blended mocha."

"With whipped cream," June added in no uncertain terms. "And a Danish."

June and Annie found some prime real estate near a window overlooking the bay and seated themselves. June slurped on her frosty, as I like to call it, and Annie did her best with the muffin that was Jack-size in proportions.

"So, tell me," Annie said, hinting at her previous question.

"They're friends, those two. Have been since they were kids. But they feud like brothers."

"Why is that?"

"Who knows? They're competitive, that's all. Rory was in love with Lily, before she fell in love with Jack," June went on, slurping and slurping. She pulled the straw from the lid and licked the whipped cream.

"Lily?"

"Jack's wife. She died some years back."

Annie put down her coffee gently and her eyes went wide with shock. That was a bit of information she hadn't heard before.

"How did she die?" Annie wondered if maybe she was asking too much. She didn't realize that in Newport, you're never asking too much.

"She was sick, I'm afraid. Had breast cancer, so many years before anyone her age should have breast cancer," June explained, her tone sad and heavy.

"That's awful." I'm pretty sure Annie didn't know what else to say.

"The whole town grieved over it, and Jack hasn't been the same since. She was a nice lady. There is no sense in what happened to her."

The two of them looked out the window again in silence. The morning had turned somber and cold, all in an instant.

"Between you, me, and the fencepost," June went on, leaning into the table and whispering. "There are some missing pieces in the puzzle between Rory and Jack."

"Oh?"

"Sure, you know. Lily did love Rory, and they had a fine relationship, but once he introduced her to Jack – she was from out of town, you see, from Maine – but once he introduced her to Jack, her affections changed. Rory let her go, like a man of true integrity. But he always sensed that Jack didn't love her as much as he did. She wanted to move back to Maine and Jack saw a ticket out of this place. You know, a proper explanation for leaving, otherwise his mother would have killed him. But after Lily died, I think Rory held onto the belief that if she were with him, it wouldn't have happened."

"But how is that possible?"

"I guess he just thought that love would kill the cancer. And happiness. In fact, Rory didn't believe that Jack loved Lily at all."

Chills went up and down Annie's spine.

****

"You can't be afraid of raw bacon if you're going to make chowder, Annie," I said, seeing the terror on her face.

"Tony, I've never touched raw bacon in my life."

"And so, you've never lived."

It was a rare occasion for me. I was teaching someone how to cook. And not just any someone, but my Annie. Mine, mine, mine. Okay, I'm joking.

But she was in the kitchen of the SharkFin, Josephine was off in the distance scowling as she breaded the fish for our famous fish and chips, and I was showing Annie how to make chowder from scratch. It all happened out of the blue. It was the evening after Christmas and Annie was back at the SharkFin for a whiskey. The conversation turned to chowder, and there we found ourselves.

I barked. "Throw it in the pot."

"Like this?" Annie placed the pieces of bacon into the pan.

"Yes, that's what you call 'throwing it in the pot.' Now, put the onions in there."

Annie protested. "Tony, my eyes are watering. I can't see."

"It's from the onions. You'll get used to it."

Tears were streaming down her face. "Oh god."

"Now, we're going to let that crisp up for five minutes and then we're going to add the water and cubed potatoes."

"You're so serious when you're cooking," Annie said with a tearful smile.

"This is serious business, kid." I was eyeing the pot like a chemist eyes a petri dish.

I gotta show you something here, except you can't see it with your own eyes. But paint the picture if you can:

Annie wore an apron with a huge red lobster on it, her cheeks were also red from the heat, and tears were streaming down her face. These were tears of oniony joy.

"It was a beautiful day today, now wasn't it?" I said with pride, enjoying pleasant small talk while the bacon sizzled.

"Gorgeous. I took June to Barringer's for breakfast."

"I hope you enjoyed the sunshine coming in through those windows. A storm is brewing tomorrow." I wasn't taking my eyes off the onions. They were just getting brown.

"Oh no." Annie frowned. "I'm supposed to go out on the water tomorrow."

"What?"

"Yes, Rory asked if I would go."

Okay, I had to think about a thing or two in that moment. First of all, the onions were done and I desperately needed to put in the potatoes, but simultaneously, I needed to ask Annie about the future rendezvous, because it troubled me. I decided that the issue with Rory could wait for ten seconds.

"Put in the potatoes!" I cried.

"God, so urgent." Annie did as I told her to do.

"That's better." I felt a calm come over me. Like all was right in the world again. Except for the Rory issue. "So, he asked you out again, huh?"

"Yes, I think that he's a nice guy. But I was talking with June today, about Rory and Jack…and Lily."

There was apprehension in her voice, and I could tell why. If June had told her everything that I think she told her – because June has a wagging tongue – then it all made perfect sense.

I stirred the pot. "That was quite a situation there."

"It seems like it," Annie replied.

"Salt and pepper!"

"Okay, okay." Annie tossed it in.

I threw the lid on the pot. "Now, while those soften, we can talk."

"Do you think Jack was in love with Lily?"

Boy, did she open a can of warms.

"In his way."

"What's that supposed to mean?"

"I mean he cared for her, and she was madly in love with him."

"But did he love her?"

I paused. I was treading on rough water and I didn't want to capsize the ship before butter and cream were added to the soup.

"Ya know, kid. I'm not sure." I was being blatantly honest. Annie deserved no less. The time that Jack and Lily were together was also the time that he and I were talking the least. I was heavily into my cups at that point as well, so my senses weren't keen, to say the least. I regret that, I must admit. I was absent at several points in Jack's life when he needed me most.

"Fair enough." Annie didn't want to press me further. She didn't feel like it was her business, I imagine. But she was intrigued by Jack. More than intrigued; and that's why she asked as much as she did.

In the fifteen minutes of precious waiting that followed, I wanted to reassure Annie. I wanted to tell her that the history between Jack and Rory wasn't as dire as it seemed.

But mostly, I wanted to tell her to not get on that boat with Rory tomorrow, for reasons that I didn't yet know.

I pontificated. "Sometimes walking through the lives of Newporters is like walking on a sandy beach. It's pleasant and serene, but there's a good chance that you're going to step on a piece of glass."

"Or you could find buried treasure," Annie said with a smile.

Looked like things were perking up in Annie's life, after all. For once, she was the optimist among us.

I cried with urgency. "Half and half!"

"Okay, okay." Annie dumped the contents of the measuring cup into the pot.

"Butter," I added with profundity.

"How much?"

"The whole shebang." I was insulted that she even asked.

"The whole stick of butter?"

"Don't blame me. We ran out. It's usually more."

So, I watched as Annie added the butter, wincing all the while, followed by the clams, and then the clam juice. It smelled like oceanic, dairy farm heaven, and it would be ready in only five minutes.

As Annie looked down into the chowder, the aroma overtook her and she closed her eyes in pleasure. When she reopened them, I could see that the issue of Rory and Jack had escaped her, at least for a brief moment.

Chapter 12

There are one or two ways that I can tell the next part of this story, because it's really a book unto itself. But what you need to know is that the following morning, when Annie got on that ship with Rory, not only was she apprehensive about the amorous look in his eye, she also couldn't deny the black clouds overhead.

Despite the weather reports, Rory was a man with a mission and therefore undeterred. He saw it as his big chance. I can say this with some clarity because I'm a man and I understand how the brain operates in these situations. Rory would helm the ship intrepidly, the pelting rain barraging his face while Annie clutched him, feeling his warmth, gaining strength from, well…his intrepidness.

She'd feel fear as the waves crashed all around them, but once he brought them safe to harbor, Annie would be flushed with pride over how Rory had handled the situation.

That was not what happened.

What did happen was that, yes, the rain started pelting down, the waves crashed all around them, the engine died, and Rory was at a loss for what to do. His damn radio didn't even work. It was a disaster. Annie was filled with fear, clutching at the cockpit of the vessel, not Rory, and watching as her life flashed before her eyes.

Rory showed no fear. "I'm going to fix this."

"Please," Annie said under her breath, thinking that she didn't wish to be the Natalie Woods of Newport.

Annie felt sick, and I don't blame her. If you've never been caught in a storm like that on a mid-size vessel, then you simply can't understand. The feeling is like nothing you've ever experienced before.

"Control Center," Rory said into the radio. "Control Center," he repeated in vain, pressing a number of buttons and still hearing nothing. "Mayday."

Annie feared for the worst. "Oh, please don't say mayday." She knew nothing about sailor jargon but definitely knew that mayday was a bad sign.

"Everything is under control."

"You already said that!" Annie screamed over the sound of waves and wind.

Just then, Rory looked off to a bright light on his right. It was so hazy they couldn't even see the lighthouse, let alone the shore, but there was a distinct, bright light coming towards them which just had to be another ship.

"Probably the harbor patrol," Rory called out to her.

Inside, Annie was saying a prayer that it was indeed the harbor patrol.

The light got closer and closer, and the vessel that approached also made its presence known with a rather loud horn. Rory was reassured at first, until he realized that the boat that was drawing near was Jack's.

"Shit," Rory said under his breath.

"Is it the harbor patrol?"

"No. It's not."

Not only had Jack come out on his own boat, but he had a small team of guys with him, including Gregor, in order to facilitate matters. They quickly managed to pull their boat along the starboard side of Rory's and created a link so that the two beleaguered passengers could hop boats.

Gregor's voice cried out through the howls of the storm. "Come on!" The Russian threw out his hands, hoping to bring Annie aboard first.

"Go!" Rory cried, encouraging her.

Annie was terrified. "Aren't you coming?"

"I'm staying with the ship. Gonna get it to work," Rory called back.

"Don't be stupid," Gregor hollered. "Leave it. It's too dangerous."

"No, I can get it to work!"

Just then, before she knew what hit her, Annie saw someone forcefully kick open the door of the cockpit, vigorously grabbing her hand and pulling her aboard the other ship, then hopping onto Rory's ship. It all happened within a blink of an eye. Only after she was safely in the cockpit did she realize that the figure was Jack.

She watched as the two men screamed at each other on Rory's boat, but couldn't hear a word that they said through the storm that raged between them. Annie watched helplessly as their ship slowly idled away.

Gregor took the wheel and tried to angle the boat back towards Rory's. "Pull up to them again."

"They're drifting," another man yelled.

"We have to get closer," Gregor said.

The turning of the wheel took incredible force and Gregor heaved from the difficulty of it. Finally, he managed to turn the boat and lead it back into Rory's. What happened next was an image that Annie would not soon forget.

Not content to leave Rory alone to die on his ship, Jack picked his friend up and threw him over his shoulder like a sack of potatoes, then hopped back onto his boat, kicking Rory's boat away.

Annie watched through the glass as the two men, both lying down on the pummeled deck, continued to argue and wail at one another. To this day, Annie didn't know what they were screaming about. She thought Jack might have been scolding Rory for going into such danger and bringing Annie with him.

But to be honest with you, they were screaming about a lot more than that. And all those words disappeared amidst the wind and the rain, never to be retrieved again.

In the wake of that traumatic afternoon, Annie did something that she'd been holding off for exactly one week: she returned her rental car. Why and how did she do that, you ask? She had been perusing the classified section of the Newport Herald. It was something she'd been working on most mornings; looking at the cheap cars. The jalopies, as I like to call them, and the affordable apartments, of which there were few.

But sure enough, the day after her three-hour tour at sea, Annie made things happen. The car was an old Nissan Maxima, which, if you ask me, was a pretty luxurious car in its day, but when Annie met her – cars are always 'hers' – for the first time, she could tell that it was a bag of bones.

That being said, it moved. It might cost Annie a fortune down the line, but for $600, she wasn't complaining.

Returning the rental car was a mixed experience. She left the Maxima at Newport Hollows and had June drive her to the rental place half an hour away. Annie said goodbye to ole' Blue, the car that had helped her escape Cosmopolitan death, and that was that.

The next order of business – and I kid you not, this was in the very same day – was to drive to a little house by the water that had a room for rent. It was Cheryl and Johnny Bigalow's place. It wasn't anything fancy, but Cheryl had taken pains to convert one of the bottom rooms into its own one-bedroom apartment. She said she did it for the extra income because she refused to do that 'Airbnb crap,' as she called it.

Annie stepped one foot into that apartment and knew it was the one. The rent was cheap, it looked out over the water, and there was a painting of a mermaid in the bedroom. Those things, coupled with the fact that it was fully furnished, and Annie finally had her own place. Let me tell you, when Annie decides to get things done, she gets things done.

Apparently, someone was knocking at Cheryl's door, so she left Annie alone in the place for a few minutes as she went to see who it was. In that brief time, Annie took a deep breath and felt peace. She told me about it. She just knew that it was the place for her. Annie was convinced that good things were going to happen there.

It ended up being more complicated than that, but we'll get there when we get there.

So, Annie was getting all settled in Newport. I don't have to tell you that I couldn't have been happier. Annie was hugging herself inside, but that's when thoughts of the bigwig came to mind.

There was something about breaking free, about making a change and doing things on her own, which made her miss the guy. I hate to even talk about it, but that's how things work, you know. Annie wanted to know what he'd think of the place. If he'd be proud of her. She even wanted him to see it and enjoy the victory of sharing her view, pouring a glass of wine together, all that crap.

Annie knew better than that, but still she couldn't help but let her mind wander. And I don't blame her. She was in love with the guy.

And the bastard was still in Paris.

But back to happier topics. Things were truly looking up for my girl.

Cheryl made a hasty return. "You can move in anytime you like." She wore a Christmas lightbulb necklace, but several of the bulbs had already died.

"I think I'll swing by tomorrow, then." Annie hated to leave June. Yet ultimately, the prospect of not having to face someone every day, first thing in the morning, just to get your coffee, had become very appealing.

"That's fine." Cheryl twirled her necklace in her fingers. "We'll leave the door open."

"And I'll write a check," Annie said quickly, wanting to reassure Cheryl that she actually had money. As luck would have it, she didn't need to, 'cause June had already spoken with Cheryl over the phone and vouched for Annie's character.

"No rush." Cheryl always hated to talk about money. "And let us know if you need anything."

When Annie left her new place on Fisherman Street, she was light as air. Nothing could stop her now. Except, that is, when her car didn't start.

"Shit." She turned the ignition again and again. Nothing doing.

Annie paused and took a breath. Surely, getting too riled up about it wouldn't do a thing. Rightfully, from my perspective, her first thought was to call Jack. Sadly, she didn't have his number in her phone. The next bet was to call Rory, and his number *was* in her phone.

Moral of the story: don't leave your fate in your phone.

Rory was there in no time. He'd already recovered from the previous day's tempest, but his boat hadn't.

"I'm sorry about what happened," Rory said penitently as he looked under Annie's hood.

"Don't worry about it. How were we supposed to know that it would get that bad?" Annie felt bad for the guy. Surely, his pride was more than a little hurt.

"You feeling okay today?"

"Fine. I was frozen to the bone when I got back to the B&B, but June made me a hot toddy."

"That's what I could have used." Rory gave an apologetic laugh.

"How's it looking?" Annie asked, her brow knit.

"Just some low fluids. I'll get the stuff from my trunk and it'll be as good as new."

"I can't thank you enough."

"It's always my pleasure, Annie." Rory looked at her

116

for an inordinate amount of time before returning to his truck. For whatever reason, the way he was starting to look at her made her uneasy.

Chapter 13

That night, it was just a table for two; June and Annie, sitting by the window and yet again watching the snowfall. The Christmas tree of Newport Hollows was still up. June wouldn't dream of getting rid of it till after New Year's.

"You didn't have to cook," Annie said.

"It's my favorite lasagna. I'm trying to fatten you up before you go. God only knows if you'll feed yourself properly," June said, a box of tissue beside her. Yes, the old bird was shedding some tears. Annie had only been there two weeks and already they were like peas in a pod.

"I'm just moving down the street, June." Annie took a dainty bite of the gooey lasagna. I mean, gooey in the good way. Not the gross way.

"Promise you'll come back for pancakes every Sunday," June said, blowing her nose into a tissue.

Annie lifted her hand in the air. "You have my word of honor."

"There's a housewarming party tomorrow night," June said matter-of-factly.

"Where?"

"At your place."

"There is?"

"Sure. No one told you? As soon as Cheryl called me with the news, I called up all the ladies from the book club and the Newport Mansion Society."

"June!" Annie protested. "My place is tiny."

"We'll spill over into the main house if we have to." June gloomily poured herself another glass of chianti and tore off another piece of garlic bread.

"Well, it's too much. You shouldn't have." Although she'd be annoyed if anyone else had pulled that one on her, Annie was happy that the ladies would be joining her the next night. They'd make lovely housewarming guests, indeed.

"Even Samantha will be there. Every once in a while, that kid takes breaks from saving the world."

"I would like to live in a world ruled by Samantha," Annie said lovingly, thinking of the girl with the horn-rimmed glasses who had Jane Eyre all figured out.

"I invited Jack, too."

"You what?" Annie put down her fork.

"He'll be the lone rooster in the henhouse. If he shows up. He's very mercurial, you know."

"You didn't have to do that, June," Annie said, feeling a blush come to her cheek.

"Well, I know you fancy each other."

Annie was silent for a moment. Sure, she fancied Jack, but was there any conceivable way that he felt the same? It was certainly hard to tell.

I could have told her, of course. I could have sat her down with a strong whiskey and informed her that Jack was crazy about her. Crazier than he'd ever been for a lady in some time.

Annie protested. "We've known each other for such a short amount of time."

"Sometimes, that's all that it takes."

But still, there was the whole Rory issue. It was weirding Annie out enough that she had to talk to June about it.

"I think Rory is pursuing me," Annie said, taking a bite of garlic bread. There was enough butter on it to sink a ship.

"Duh!" June exclaimed. "He's taken you out on the boat two times now. No man takes a lady out on his boat two times without having intentions."

"But the second time, the boat nearly sank. Maybe that's a bad omen."

If I could have, I would have told her just that. Yes. It was a bad omen. Run.

"And Jack came and saved the day," June said dreamily.

"How did you know that?" Annie didn't recall telling June that bit of the story.

"Honey, it's a small town. Everyone knows everything. It's just like Jack to save the day. He's that type."

The intention was to drive home the same thing that I wanted to drive home. I guess June and I were in cahoots, but we just didn't know it.

Annie sighed. "Well, thank god he was there. Who knows what would have happened."

She became introspective, thinking of the possibility of Jack stepping foot into her new apartment the following night. What the heck was that going to be like? She imagined it would be quite nice, actually.

"Well, I have a whole other lasagna for you to take," June said, blowing her nose one last time and getting up from the table.

"A whole lasagna?"

"Yes, a whole one. Just make sure none of the guests see it tomorrow night. This lasagna is for you and you alone," June said in no uncertain terms. "Or in case Jack wants to hang around after the party and needs a snack." June winked before disappearing into the kitchen.

Annie shook her head in dismay. No doubt, she wouldn't even have to worry about food for the party, because June was going to cater the whole thing. She'd need to clean, of course, and maybe set up some decorations. Mostly, she just wanted her place to have the good juju that she needed in her life.

At the very least, she hoped the guests would bring the good juju if what was there wasn't enough. That's what housewarming parties were all about, anyway.

"Here you are." June brought out a casserole dish that was the size of the SS Constitution.

"Oh my god." Annie thought she'd have to cut it into pieces and store it in the freezer. It would probably last till next Christmas.

"Now, let me help you carry your bags to the car," June said.

"I only have one bag, June."

"You've got more than that. I have boxes of dishware that I'm giving you. Haven't used any of it in years. I've also got some extra toilet paper and tissue papers from the Bargain Shopper."

Annie cocked her head to one side and smiling warmly. "You don't need to do that."

"Of course, I do. Your bum and your nose will thank me."

And so, car packed, Annie left Newport Hollows and shed a few tears herself as she waved goodbye. She was going to miss her first home in Newport, but at least she knew she always had a key.

And she could count on June showing up at her place nearly every single day.

That night, Annie went to her new home and was filled with wonder, as one always is when they're beginning afresh. She looked out her window, seeing the lighthouse off in the distance and the graceful moon overhead. The moonlight broke into countless little pieces across the water and Annie knew that she picked the right place.

The chianti, lasagna, and garlic bread made for a restful sleep, and when Annie awoke the next morning, she thought she was in a dream. At first, she had to remind herself where she was. The clouds overhead were dark and silvery, and the water was grey and menacing, but not without charm. The landscape was beautiful in its cold, white darkness. She saw fishing boats out in the harbor, and for a brief moment, she wondered if Jack might be on one of those boats, leaving for Maine. The thought made her heart sink.

There was a lot to do, but almost none of it involved unpacking her one small duffle bag. She wanted to clean the place until it was spotless. There were some cobwebs here, some dust bunnies there, and a few dead bugs to and fro, but aside from that, Annie decided the place was in tip-top condition and ready for guests.

She bought wine for the party, enough to satisfy the tainted livers of the book club, and she also made cookies. Now, I'm not talking from-scratch cookies. I'm saying the ones that come in a tube that you cut into disks, but at least she made an effort. Annie thought there would be nothing more enchanting than a house party that smelt of Nestle Tollhouse.

The rest of the day was spent writing, of course. More crap jobs that Annie wouldn't even tell me about. In later years, she explained that she once wrote product descriptions for an industrial goods website in Canada. Fans of her books still love that story. And about the time when she wrote quizzes for retirement communities.

Day turned into night, as it always does, and before she knew it, Annie had guests upon her. They came in droves – because they all carpooled. Half of them couldn't drive at night – and each one came with a dish of some sort to be shared by all. Others brought housewarming gifts that Annie might find useful. Myrtle brought an Afghan throw that she had knitted 'by hand.' Peggy brought a very expensive vase which made June cringe.

"That was probably made in China," June protested.

"It's a rare Chinese artifact. Of course, it was made in China," was Peggy's rebuttal.

Gayle, ever-jolly, brought a large wheel of cheese. No crackers, no condiments, just cheese. She said it was an Italian tradition.

Samantha, bless her heart, brought a fresh copy of Gloria Steinem's "Revolution from Within," and the rest of the guests brought candles, picture frames, scented soap, and the like.

The place was booming with sexagenarian and septuagenarian women who knew how to have a good time once the box of Pinot Grigio was opened, and everyone stuffed their faces with food.

And when I say there was a lot of food, I mean there was a lot of food. Someone even brought a three-tiered cake which put Annie's cookies to shame.

"To Annie's new life!" June said, raising her paper cup for a toast.

All the ladies cheered. "To Annie's new life!"

If the meaning of a housewarming party was just that, to warm the house with love and laughter, then the mission was accomplished on that evening. Annie couldn't believe her luck at having so many fast friends.

I knew about the party. Heard about it. Even got an invitation. But I wasn't going to be the first rooster to step into that henhouse, and I was pretty sure that I would have been, because Jack showed up late.

The knock was heard on the door at 9 pm. Keep in mind, that would have been early to arrive at any other party, but the old birds at Annie's place were seriously winding down at that point. A few of them fell asleep off in the corner. The knock was different than any other one she heard that night, because it was robust and well…manly.

Rushing to the door, Annie opened it and felt her heart drop out of her chest, onto the floor, rolling down the hill and into the marina, where it sank to death in happiness. Okay, that was perhaps a bit too much, but Jack was at the door.

"Hey, Annie," he said, holding up a modest bouquet of flowers. In fact, it was the most modest gift she had received that night, and Annie was thankful for that.

"Hey, Jack, come in." Annie congenially ushered him into his worst nightmare. Okay, that isn't fair to the old birds, but you can imagine Jack's terror at seeing so many empty boxes of Pinot Grigio.

"Jack, you came," June exclaimed, rushing up to him with open arms.

"Of course." He accepted June's bear-like embrace. The woman had always been a crusher more than a hugger.

"For me?" she exclaimed, taking the flowers from Jack's hand.

"No, for Annie."

"I know that, silly. I was just teasing you. Here you go, Annie." June handed her the flowers and gave her a wink.

"Thanks, these are beautiful," Annie said, bringing them to her nose.

"Okay girls, party's over." June clapped her hands and commanded the room. All the ladies perked up – well, honestly, they perked up when Jack arrived – but June's clapping perked them up further. "Time to move."

So, like a general, June got those ladies out of the joint as fast as immigrants move when seeing police at the border. Sorry for the analogy. After all the commotion was done, all the cheek-kissing and well-wishes, Jack and Annie were left alone.

Chapter 14

"Are you hungry? There's lasagna." Annie was unsure of how else to begin. June had made a massive tray of it, after all.

Jack took a look around the place. "That sounds nice."

"I'll warm it up in the microwave, if that's okay."

"Fine by me. I'm used to the microwave." Jack walked around the apartment, inspecting things.

This made Annie feel a little funny at first, like her new home was being investigated by a police officer, but later she would come to understand that Jack was checking to make sure the walls were well-built, the electrics were up to snuff, and the piping would withstand the frigid Newport winters. In all of those things, he was satisfied, but I know that he secretly hoped that something would be broken so that he could offer to help.

Guys like to be of help to a lady, and Jack was no exception.

"I'm afraid I don't have anything else to go with it except for chocolate chip cookies," Annie said from the kitchen. "Everything else was devoured by the book club."

"Voracious appetites, those ladies."

"And voracious minds, I'll have you know," Annie added, pulling out plates and dishing up the lasagna.

Okay, so she overheated it in the microwave. The cheese turned to glue and the vegetables were incinerated, but Jack wouldn't care. Next time, I'd tell them to come to me for lasagna. I wouldn't even trust June's, and that's saying a lot.

"Here we go." Annie handed Jack a plate.

Just as she was walking back to the kitchen to get things to set the table with, she found that Jack followed her, reached for a fork from a drawer, and began to eat, standing in the kitchen.

It was a teaching moment for Annie. It wasn't that Jack didn't have manners, he was just used to eating while standing in his kitchen. On the boat, he'd eat in the cockpit using a plastic spork.

"Do you want to sit down?"

"Oh," Jack replied, realizing that he had perhaps made a mistake. "Yes."

So, Annie set the modest table, which was about the size of a high school desk, and the two of them sat, enjoying their decimated lasagna and looking out towards the water.

"It was so nice of you to come," Annie said.

"It's my pleasure."

Yes, he was a man of few words, but those two truly enjoyed each other's company, even in the silence. Annie was so happy she didn't even think to pour them two glasses of wine. It became obsolete when one already felt that warm, tingly feeling all over.

"So, you're here to stay?" Jack demolished his lasagna in two minutes flat.

"I guess it's official. There's something about this place. I don't know. I feel more peaceful."

"Well, you have no history here. So, yeah, I can see how it might be peaceful." Of course, Newport was anything but peaceful for him, for reasons I have already clumsily explained.

"I need to thank you again. For the other day. On the boat."

Annie was treading on sensitive waters, but she still needed to say it. It was the second time Jack had shown a feat of heroism in her presence.

"It was nothing. I've seen that kind of thing before."

"You weren't scared?" Annie asked.

"I'm never scared on the water. If the sea is going to take me, it's going to take me."

"I find that hard to believe."

"Don't," Jack said, wiping his mouth with his napkin and then taking a good, hard look at her. It made Annie self-conscious at first, until she realized that he was staring because he admired what he saw.

Annie didn't wish to make a comparison to the bigwig in New York, but she couldn't help it. That guy had a lot of words – was stuffed to the gunnels with them – and never lived up to a one. Jack was different. He promised nothing, but I tell you, he had a lot to deliver.

"Why don't you come over to the house, for New Year's?" Jack said.

So, that was beyond bold. He was offering to have Annie over to the house, just the two of them, for quite an important holiday. She was aware of his intentions, and the invitation was one that she couldn't refuse.

"I would love that," Annie replied, not wanting to sound as enthusiastic as she felt.

"Great." I know that he was relieved that she said yes. In fact, I know that it cost him a great deal just to ask. "Casual. You can wear your PJs if you like." Jack smiled.

"Then maybe I will."

As the two were clearing dishes, feeling satisfied with how the evening had gone, and just how damn comfortable they were around one another, a sound outside of Annie's front door gave her a start.

"What was that?" Annie asked, turning off the faucet.

"I don't know." Jack went to the door to investigate. He seemed nonplussed, but Annie's heart was pounding. He opened the door, and outside in the darkness stood a figure.

"Hey."

"Hey." Jack was leaning against the doorframe like he owned the place. He can be cocky, too, just so you know.

"I just wanted to congratulate Annie." Rory stepped closer to the door.

"It's kind of late for that, Rory."

With that, he wasn't trying to be cocky. It truly was too late.

Rory was clearly a little intoxicated. "I was at another party and lost track of time."

"Maybe you should go home and sleep it off."

"Can I say hello to Annie first?" Rory poked his head around Jack and waved to Annie. "I'm going to sneak past your bodyguard for a moment and give you a hug." He performed the maneuver just as he described it.

Annie opened her arms and embraced him. Rory was a friend of hers, after all. The hug was a long one, and Annie

129

tried to pull away after it got to the awkward point, but Rory wouldn't let go.

"I'm so proud of you," Rory whispered in her ear.

All during this display of affection, Jack just stood there. There was nothing else he could do.

"I'll be off before my friend kills me." Rory pulled away and gave Jack a hearty pat on the back.

"See you, Rory," Jack said flatly.

"See you, bud." Rory looked deep into Jack's eyes. I didn't have to be there to know what those glances meant. Rory was telling Jack to get out of his way, and Jack was telling Rory to back off. It was accomplished without words.

Once Rory had gone, Jack was left with a conundrum. He didn't want to intrude upon Annie's space much longer, but he also didn't want to leave her alone.

"You going to be okay?" Jack asked.

"Of course. Is there something I don't know?"

"No..." Jack considered his words. Instead of explaining more, he grabbed a pen and paper that were set on the kitchen counter and quickly wrote down his cell number. Next, he tested the lock on Annie's door, and finally he was satisfied, but just barely. "Call if you have any problems. I'm just minutes away."

"Thanks, Jack. I'll be fine." Annie walked him to the door.

They desperately wanted to kiss each other. There was an electric pull between them, but Jack didn't want to offend her and Annie didn't want to make any assumptions. Instead, they embraced and held each other, more briefly than the embrace with Rory, and much more powerful.

Annie disappeared into his chest and Jack liked having her there.

"Goodnight, Annie."

"Goodnight, Jack."

She closed the door and locked it behind him, then looked down at the scribbled phone number, wondering why Jack thought it was so urgent.

As Annie lay in bed that night, she was flattered by Jack's protectiveness, but she still didn't understand the reason for it.

That was, until the next day, when Annie awoke to find withered flowers on her doorstep and a slew of texts from Rory asking why Jack was at her house, why she hadn't defended him, and how it was that she could be interested in two best friends at once.

Annie was horrified, and for obvious reasons. She considered telling Jack, but she thought that would be absurd. She wanted to tell June, but then the whole town would know what had happened. Annie was resolved that she'd only tell me, which I approved of, but it would take a few days before Annie would do so.

Instead, all that next day, she decorated her apartment, cleaned, did some work, and locked her doors. Annie couldn't bring herself to answer Rory's texts because it all seemed so absurd. But at the end of the day, this negligence only added fuel to the fire, which I could've warned her about had she told me sooner.

Instead of worrying, or responding to Rory, Annie planned out in her mind what she'd wear for New Year's at Jack's, and also what she'd bring. She could cook, but that would be a disaster. Maybe she could pick something up for the two of them to enjoy instead of microwave dinners?

A thought came to mind. Annie remembered a brochure that had been on her bedside table at Newport Hollows; the picture of a technicolor aquarium complete with treasure chest and glittery mermaid. It was the menu for King's Palace, haute Chinese cuisine of Newport. As I mentioned, it was just American Chinese food, but it did hold some glamor, and Annie decided there would be nothing more fitting her first New Year's in Newport than to order some Chinese food, and perhaps wear her PJs.

She considered her choice for a moment, but what guy didn't like Chinese food?

In the days leading up to the big event, Annie got more cozy in her place and Rory became much more insistent. The crazy texts continued, things were placed at her door, and Annie wondered what the heck to do. She'd have to confront him, of course. Tell him that he needed to calm down and that he was overreacting. If she knocked some sense into him, then perhaps he'd understand.

You know that I love Annie, but I want to kick her for those days when she said nothing, all the while, Rory's craziness was brewing. If she had told me, or better yet, told Jack, then maybe it wouldn't have come to a head the way that it did.

But we're not there yet in the story and as you know, I hate to jump ahead.

So, suffice it to say that, even though the situation was no good, Annie woke up one morning and found that it was New Year's Eve. She already had the items that she was going to order checked off on the King's Palace brochure menu.

So, she showed up in her PJs. Annie thought it was pretty embarrassing that the pants had rainbows and unicorns on them, but she figured that Jack might as well see the truth. She was a dweeb. Do people even use that word anymore?

She had ordered enough food from King's Palace to feed an army. There was a large plastic bag in each hand, and the smell was to-die-for, in Annie's estimation. Even though she assumed that Jack would be impressed by the sheer size and scope of her order, when he opened the door at Leavenworth, Jack didn't even bat an eye.

Jack grabbed the bags from her hands. "Here, let me take those."

"You're not wearing PJs," Annie said, filled with more than a little bit of shame in her own outfit.

"I don't wear PJs." Jack led her through the long entrance hall to the back kitchen.

As he walked, Annie was naturally mortified, but she was also taking in the view from behind. I don't mean to be crass, but Jack was wearing a tailored pair of jeans, white t-shirt, and leather shoes. Annie thought that he looked edible, but she'd never admit that to anyone. Who could blame her? Jack was a good-looking kid.

Looking down at her unicorn pajama bottoms in shame, Annie shook her head.

"You should've called me and told me that you were joking about the PJs."

"Come on," Jack replied, turning to her, "you look great."

There was a sparkle in Jack's eye and it made Annie blush. Yes, he was flirting with her and she could tell.

"I got a bottle of champagne." Jack placed the two bags on the counter and opened them up to see what was inside.

"I ordered the whole restaurant."

"This is nothing. This is like, weekday dinner-size for me."

Annie noticed something very peculiar as she was in that enormous kitchen, oddly vacant considering the size of it. She was nervous. Now, it wasn't like Annie to be self-conscious and nervous in social situations. I mean, everyone gets that once in a while. But it was the presence of Jack that did something to her whole body. There was something different about him. He wasn't dark and moody, secretive, and silent. Jack was bright and shiny on that night. Happy and open. He was like a polished penny, and for whatever reason, it scared the crap out of Annie.

If you ask me, I think it's because there was no barrier between them. There was no defensiveness. They were two people, deeply interested in one another, and standing in the same kitchen.

Jack laughed. "I can give you a pair of pants, if you want to change."

"No, no." Annie waved away the idea. "I'm comfy, actually."

"I think that we should eat this right away." Jack pulled two plates from an overhead cupboard.

They went into the dining room, which was hilarious because it was basically built for large parties. Annie expertly arranged the paper cartons of Chinese food on the sideboard, Jack set the table, and wine was poured.

A huge chandelier hung over the table, and Jack flipped the switch so that it illuminated the cavernous room with sparkling white light.

Annie looked up at the dome-like white ceiling. "This is so formal."

"Yes, everything except the *lo mein* and the PJs."

"These are my fanciest pajama bottoms, I'll have you know."

And so, they ate their cuisine, sipped their wine, and talked about the house, their plans for the New Year, their mutual love of the sea, and many other topics that filled them both with a kind of relaxed wellbeing. What they did not talk about, even for a moment, was Rory.

"You know about the fireworks?" Jack asked.

"No." Annie cracked open her fortune cookie. She always had a thing for those fateful treats. Annie believed that what they said was true. Sometimes, with the really good ones, she'd tape them on her fridge.

"There are fireworks over the lighthouse, at midnight." Jack opened his cookie, as well.

"How exciting."

"We'll watch it on the porch."

Annie barely heard Jack's suggestion because she was too enthralled by her fortune.

Love will transform your life.

Now, I gotta say here that, with her overactive imagination, Annie had to wonder whether or not it was a plant. Not the kind that grows in your yard, but the other kind. She'd heard stories about men going to all kinds of lengths to plant fortune cookies with predetermined sayings. Of course, she knew that she was overthinking it

135

but the notion brought a smile to Annie's face. And alas, it was impossible because she was the one that bought the food.

"*Money will flow into your life.*" Jack tossed it aside.

"You're not going to keep it?" Annie thought it crazy of him to disregard such a good fortune.

"It's just a piece of paper."

"You should put it in your wallet."

"I can't actually use it as money, Annie."

The two of them laughed, and Jack asked Annie what her fortune was. Filled with embarrassment about reading it aloud, Annie refused. What followed was a kind of game that lasted until midnight. Jack would try to wrench the fortune from her hand, Annie would run and scream, and they'd chase each other around the mansion like two kids.

Tired, out of breath, and happy, Annie and Jack ended up on the porticoed balcony at midnight, looking out over a vast sea of white hills and black ocean.

Other partygoers could be heard at nearby homes, counting down and cheering. Sure enough, when the clock struck midnight, a generous array of fireworks launched over the water, leading people to cheer and blow horns.

Before Annie even knew what was happening, she found herself in Jack's arms, her lips pressed against his. It was a stealthy attack on Jack's part. He just swooped right in. I think that he could have been a bit more of a gentleman about it, but Annie said she was more than happy that he did.

It was the greatest kiss of her life. She told me as much.

Chapter 15

"Why didn't you show him the fortune?" I asked.

Annie sipped her whiskey. "'Cause it just seemed so corny."

It was New Year's Day. The SharkFin was actually pretty quiet, but I was used to that on January 1st. Most folks were with their families, or nursing hangovers at home. That's why it came as a pleasant surprise when Annie came walking through the door. It was even more gratifying for me when she started telling me the whole story of the night before.

"There's nothing corny about love." I gave the bar a good swipe with my handy towel.

"Who says it's love?"

I didn't respond to that because I damn well knew it was love and didn't want to tread upon a gentle topic. Also, considering my relation to Jack, it didn't make sense for me to pry too much.

Just then, Annie's phone beeped and she turned to check it. There was confusion on her face, and frustration, so I knew that the person trying to reach her couldn't possibly be Jack.

"What is it?" I wasn't liking that sour expression on Annie's pretty face.

"Oh, it's nothing." She put the phone away, just as it started to beep again.

"Someone bothering you?" I was ready to beat someone up if I had to. I may have had old man arms, but they could still throw a punch.

"If I tell you, can you keep a secret?"

"No," I replied. Hey, I was just being honest.

"Then I won't tell you."

"Come on, I'm joking with you. When it comes to you, I can muster up the strength to keep a secret." I leaned my elbow against the bar. Again, I was telling the truth.

"It's Rory." Her voice turned hushed and apprehensive. No, I didn't like that one bit. But as you know, I saw that situation coming from a mile away.

"I think you should tell Jack."

"There's no reason to." Annie sipped the drink.

Now, I know why she didn't want to tell him, and that was because she didn't want to just go ahead and assume that he had feelings for her. If I could have knocked some sense into her, I would have. Jack literally swooped her up into his arms the night before, on New Year's, with fireworks and cheering and all that crap. Annie should have known better.

"I'll have a word with him," I replied, not wanting to stand by another minute while Annie was being pestered by some crazy, confused, lost jerk.

"You promised you'd keep a secret!"

"Damn." I conceded, seeing that she had a point. "Then you gotta promise me something."

"What's that?"

"If Rory is worrying you, or upsetting you, you do something about it."

"Okay."

"No, not just okay." I was becoming indignant. Annie was too damn nice and I needed to get the point across. "You'll do it 'cause it's the right thing to do. And you don't deserve to take anyone's shit."

So, yes. I was being very forward with Annie, but someone needed to do it. I wanted to hold onto that secret that she told me, but if things got out of hand, I wasn't sure I'd be able to hold onto that bit of information much longer.

"Can we change the subject?"

"Yes, and the subject is food." I walked back into the kitchen and returned with a piping-hot basket of onion rings. Josephine always had a fresh supply of them on-hand, if only for her own snacking pleasure.

"Eat this," I said, placing the basket in front of Annie.

"Not hungry."

"Eat."

I was being bossy with Annie. A man's gotta do what a man's gotta do.

Annie held a hot ring in her hand and took a crunchy bite. I could tell that she didn't regret it.

"Did you get kissed last night?" Annie asked.

"Me? No. I didn't even see the ball drop. Fell asleep on the couch, drunk on root beer."

Annie laughed, and it warmed my heart to see her smiling again. And eating.

"You've never even told me if you were married before."

She knew that she was opening up a can of warms, and a family-sized can from Costco at that. Not only had she never asked me about Elizabeth before, but she'd never once heard Jack talk about his mom. Having already heard the sad story about Lily, Annie didn't think it was her place to delve any further into the family pain. Maybe the onion rings emboldened her.

"Elizabeth died of cancer when Jack was a kid. I took up the bottle. Jack resented me, and the rest was history."

Jesus, I really did summarize it on that day. I thought it was easier that way. Escape the pain by laying it out cold. I mean, it was the truth, after all, just a little condensed.

I know that the irony was not lost on Annie that two of the most important women in Jack's life had died the same way. She was silent for some time after that. I changed the subject to the rather threatening incoming storm that I heard about on the news that morning.

My family story made Annie glum for the rest of the night, and well into the next day. But a lot about Jack was beginning to make sense. No wonder he kept to himself a lot, only opened up when he began to trust someone, and played his cards close to his chest. Of course, he wasn't playing his cards so close to his chest when he planted that kiss on Annie's lips. She couldn't stop thinking about that, either.

So, the book club meeting the following day came as a welcome respite from Annie's thoughts and feelings.

"I've got the booze," June said, pulling out two jumbo bottles of Pinot Grigio. Her reasoning was – I'm sure – that New Year's was the day before and that the book club might

140

as well keep the celebration alive. She was also nursing some hurt. "I miss you." June pinched Annie on the cheek.

"Oh, June. I'm right down the street."

"I know, I know," June said, shooing the thought away. "But all I got are tourists now. People from Switzerland, Germany."

Annie tried to placate June. "There's nothing wrong with tourists."

"Yes, they pay the bills. But they can't take a joke."

Annie had to laugh. What was it about Newporters and tourists? It seemed like they should be grateful for those who paid the bills. Listen, I'm as guilty of this as the rest of 'em. But once Annie experienced her first busy summer in Newport, she'd get the hint.

June offered Samantha a drink. "No, thank you. I don't drink."

"Suit yourself. More for me." June twirled her shell necklace.

Peggy stood up, gaining the room's attention. "Can I call to everyone's attention that we have a massive storm coming our way?"

"We're here to talk about books," Myrtle replied.

"How much more is there to say about Jane Eyre?" Peggy asked in frustration.

"How much more?" Myrtle was indignant. "People have been talking about it for over a century."

"My point is," Peggy went on, "they say this one is going to be really bad. So, I feel like we should make a plan to stay safe."

"What do you suggest?" June asked.

"Maybe we should all check in with one another, over the phone."

Annie held her tongue. It would make much more sense for them to text one another, but she knew that those old birds weren't biting. They'd probably approve of the suggestion to send a telegram. I don't mean to be cruel, but there's such a divide these days between the old and the young.

"I think that's a fine idea, Peggy," June said, nodding her head in approval. "We'll make a list of everyone's phone numbers and check in after the storm strikes."

Although the wine was flowing – and not the first time that wine had flowed at the Newport Public Library – a wave of tension came over the ladies. Annie didn't understand what the big deal was. It was just a storm. But being from Washington, and never having traveled north of New York City, she just didn't get it.

Just then, Annie felt her phone buzz in her pocket and didn't even need to check to know who it was. Rory wasn't backing down.

It made her consider something. In her mind, she teased the old birds for not embracing text messages, but she had to admit that Jack was much the same. Since the big kiss, there was no texting cute little hearts and puckered faces. Instead, she received a letter. She literally received a letter. When I heard of it, I was immensely proud of my boy. In my opinion, that's definitely the way to do it.

It was placed in her mailbox that morning. Written on a simple piece of lined paper, Jack said that he had a wonderful time on New Year's, that he hoped she was well-rested since their last encounter, and asked if she might be interested in visiting the lighthouse with him.

Okay, Jack had all the moves. Let's be honest. New Year's at his mansion, Chinese food in pajamas, a tour of the famous lighthouse. He was playing all the right notes. But I assure you, he wasn't doing any of that to create a good impression. Those were genuinely things that he wished to do with Annie.

Now, the last part of the letter – the postscript, as they say – mentioned the storm, as well. Jack said, if she needed anything, she should call him.

Annie was swooning, of course. And it was warranted. When was the last time that Annie came across a decent, honorable guy? From what I knew about Annie, she had never come across one in her life. Jack may as well have been a rare panda at the zoo. He was that exotic and surprising.

The book club meeting remained somber, but naturally, once the booze kept flowing, the ladies warmed up. There was no talk of books, not even for a moment. Everything was about the storm, and when the birds were suitably sauced, they decided to go around the room and share their New Year's resolutions.

"I wish to read more books," Samantha said, nodding her head dutifully.

Annie didn't want to say it, because she admired Samantha's studiousness, but she thought that maybe what Samantha needed was to read *fewer* books.

"I have to lose weight," Peggy said, her silk caftan hiding her apparent shame.

Myrtle spoke under her breath. "Yes."

143

"I'm going to open a flower shop," June said with incredible enthusiasm.

"How remarkable," Peggy smiled tightly.

When Gayle stood up, everyone expected that she was going to express her need to lose weight, as well. "I will finally clean out my closets,"

"How about you, Annie?" June noticed that she was silent.

"That's a good question." Annie heard her phone buzz in her bag once more. "I'm going to finish my book. About Paris."

All the ladies lit up with smiles, some sipped their Pinot Grigios, and others were stunned to learn that Annie had been writing a book at all.

What none of them knew was, all that time that she'd been in Newport, Annie was writing her masterpiece.

Chapter 16

Now, I like a good storm, but this was something different entirely. Annie watched from her cozy little apartment as the white clouds suffused the sky and dumped down, leaving Newport in a blanket of white that just got thicker and thicker. She sipped cocoa – which is cute if you ask me – but there was nothing cute about what happened next.

It wasn't the snow that was so much the problem. It was the wind. It blew everything sideways, and there was no chance of hopping in your car and escaping. You wouldn't be able to see anything on the road.

I was cozy as a clam in my shack. I had a full supply of root beer on hand, loads of pretzels, and plenty of frozen pizzas. That storm could've trapped me in there for weeks and I'd be fine. But it was the rest of the townies that I was worried for.

Jack would be able to explain it best, because he was the one that knew about how things were built, and how they fell apart. Leavenworth weathered the storm just fine because Jack had taken great pains to make sure it was secure. It was the other buildings that weren't up to snuff.

It's not that Newport was dilapidated or anything. There just hadn't been a storm like that in hundreds of years. I suppose today you could blame it on global warming. Just don't say that too loud unless you want to get into a heated argument with someone old.

From where Annie sat, sipping her cocoa, writing a couple chapters, then taking a break, the phone calls started to come in and the news wasn't good.

"I'm completely trapped," Myrtle said, her voice shaky.

"Well, are you okay? Is the heat working? Do you have enough supplies?" Annie asked.

"I'm okay, but Frizzle is going out of her mind." Myrtle referred to her Chihuahua.

"Well, with a name like Frizzle, what do you expect?" Annie tried to bring some humor into the storm.

"I suppose."

The next call that came in was from Peggy, who seemed as calm as a cucumber in her stately home.

"Teddy is making fresh lobster rolls." Teddy was the rich husband, and apparently, he was also a great cook. Those were all things that pissed June off even more.

"That sounds delicious." Annie practically heard Peggy's bejeweled fingers clinking against the phone.

"I'd offer to bring you some but —"

"Yes, that would be impossible."

The next incoming call was from Jack, and when Annie saw his name come up on her cellphone, she could feel her heart beating wildly in her chest.

"Are you alright?"

"Yes, getting a lot of work done."

"The apartment is okay?"

"I think so. Heat and power are still on. I have plenty of food."

"I still have leftover Chinese," Jack said humorously.

"Oh, I wouldn't eat that if I were you."

"What? It's only been two days."

"Still. I wouldn't trust it."

"I...want to thank you again," Jack said, his tone shifting, "for a great New Year's."

"No, I've been meaning to thank you," Annie stepped over to the window and looked out. Coming close to the glass, she felt the bitter cold attempting to creep in.

"I hope I wasn't too forward." Jack was implying his stolen midnight kiss.

"It wasn't too forward." Annie felt a warm flush come to her cheek. "I really enjoyed it."

I know that it was strange for Jack to have that conversation with Annie over the phone. He was an in-person sort of guy. But, something about that heavy storm broke open Jack's heart and he felt this desperate need to talk with Annie. Well, he also felt a desperate need to be close to her and comfort her, but that would require a truck that was a lot bigger than the one that he already owned.

"When this storm is done, I'll come and dig you out." All that talk about kissing was going to undo him.

"That would be amazing," Annie replied.

"Okay." A bit of silence followed. But, as with any phone conversation, the silence doesn't last for long.

"Jack."

"Yes."

"Do you miss your boat? Being out on the water?"

She'd been thinking about that a lot since I had told her about Elizabeth over onion rings. Annie wondered if it was the reason why Jack enjoyed being out on the water. She assumed that he loved the freedom of it, and the silence. The escape from heartache.

"I do miss it a lot." He, himself, was standing by the window, looking out at the same sea of white that Annie was looking at.

"At least it's giving you time to work on the house." Annie smiled. Just thinking of Leavenworth made her happy.

"Yes. That's a good thing."

Now, I'm not taking artistic license by telling you all this, you just gotta trust me. But I think that it was the first time in Jack's life that he was happy to be stuck in Newport, and at Leavenworth. For a reason that Jack couldn't explain, it finally all had some meaning to it. Annie was the cause. That much I know.

Unfortunately, what started out as a cozy evening quickly escalated to something much darker. It was 10 pm when the power went off in Annie's apartment, then the cell service was gone, and alas, she ran out of cocoa. Although the last problem was seemingly the least important, it still filled Annie with a sense of foreboding.

Of course, Annie was prepared for the power outage. She had plenty of candles on hand, and she'd purchased an extra blanket from the Budget store. The cell service, however, was something that she couldn't fix. Now, this was back in the day when people still had landlines – remember those days? – but naturally, that wasn't working either.

Seeing that there was nothing she could do, Annie wrapped herself into a burrito with all those blankets and was able to sleep through the night. She prayed to God before she fell asleep – something that I know Annie did on occasion – and she asked Him to keep everyone safe.

I do think that Annie's prayers made a difference. I'm not religious or anything. In fact, sometimes I think that God is a putz for all the crap he has put a lot of people through, but just asking for something good does make a difference. No one was hurt in that storm. At least, not physically.

"Annie," she heard a pounding at her door, viciously waking her from sleep. A wave of terror went through her as she thought that perhaps Rory was paying a call. "Annie!"

I don't want to get too saucy here, but Annie was sleeping in her birthday suit. I tell you this with the utmost respect for her. But the reason for this – yes, she did tell me – was because it created more heat under the blankets. Using body heat, you know. So, anyhow, Annie pulled herself out of bed, still holding the blankets around her like Athena in her Grecian white robes, and went to the door.

Groggy and disoriented from sleep, Annie could barely see out her window. Well, that was because it was almost entirely blocked by snow.

"Annie."

Since she was finally awake, Annie recognized it to be Jack's voice.

He pulled at the door, trying to get it open, and Jack was having a hell of a time. The door was nearly frozen shut, but he wasn't going to give up until that puppy was open. Even if he had to drive through it with his truck.

Five sharp pulls later, the thing came open and shards of ice shot out. Annie screamed, but what she saw on the

149

other side of the door warmed her heart. Jack looked like he had just come back from a hike up Mount Everest. He wore some pretty impressive gear and had a pickaxe in his hand.

Jack was slightly out of breath. "Are you alright?"

"I'm okay." Annie shielded her eyes from the blinding white exterior of her apartment.

That was when Jack saw the state of dress – or rather, undress – that Annie was in. Okay, so he stared for a little bit, against his better judgment. Could you blame him? Annie's hair was crumpled from sleep, her exposed shoulders and collarbones were a sight, and her green eyes were shining. Essentially, Jack would have dug through an iceberg the size of a cruise ship to save her.

"Come inside, you must be freezing." Annie felt embarrassed by her ensemble. In fact, even more embarrassed than she had been in the unicorn pajamas.

Jack tried to be a gentleman and look away. "You must be freezing."

"The power went off."

"It went off everywhere. I had to make a big fire." Jack inspected her apartment.

"That must have been nice." Annie was thinking that being trapped in Leavenworth with a huge fire burning would've been the better way to go. Mostly because she'd be trapped with Jack.

"It was nice." Jack met Annie's eyes. She could tell, just by that gaze, that he had wished she was there, as well.

"Did you eat the Chinese food?" Annie looked away. Something about Jack's baby blues were too intense.

"No, I took your advice." Jack cleared his throat. "Hey, I think that you should get dressed."

"Yes, I'm sorry about –" Annie began to say, looking down at herself.

"Don't be sorry, it's just that, there's some damage in town."

"What kind of damage?"

"Newport Hollows, Barringer's, the SharkFin."

An icy cold chill ran down Annie's spine as she tried to take in what she'd just heard. Damage to Newport Hollows was bad enough, but the SharkFin was really what got her.

Alright, I only said that out of self-interest.

But in all seriousness, Jack conveyed to Annie that the damage had been structural, and no one was hurt. She got a little relief from knowing that June and I were okay, but that relief quickly turned to horror when she saw what came next.

Annie's heart was pounding all the way to Newport Hollows, where she was told the worst damage had happened. Looking out the window of the truck, Annie put her hand over her mouth to stifle a gasp.

"Oh my god."

"Yeah." Jack kept his cool.

The fact of the matter was, the old roof of Newport Hollows simply couldn't withstand the storm. Thank God June had heard and sensed that there was something wrong at about 9 pm, just before the power went off. She brought the few guests that were there – German, Swiss – down into the basement and lit a nice fire. It was smart that they did that, 'cause if they hadn't, that roof would've collapsed onto their heads.

Chapter 17

"Oh June!" Annie cried, throwing out her arms to embrace her friend.

"Annie, it all came crashing down." June was in tears.

"Thank God you're safe."

"Only by the grace of God. The Swiss were unfazed." June wiped away a tear. "I guess it happens all the time in their country."

It broke my heart when I heard about what happened at Newport Hollows. Jack later told me that it was to be expected; that the structure had been precarious for some time, but June didn't see it, or pay attention to the signs. Whatever the reason, I know that June was heartbroken by what happened. Newport Hollows was her baby, it would take a very long time to rebuild, and it would cost a fortune.

"Everything happens for a reason," Annie said, rubbing June's back.

"So, they say."

Annie feared that maybe it was too soon to say such a thing, but she felt deep in her gut that there was a reason for the catastrophe and that June was strong enough to weather that storm.

Jack stepped forward. "I think that I can be of help, June."

"Oh, Jack. You have enough on your plate." June finally released Annie from her arms.

"I'm not going to let you say no, June."

To that, June had no response, but a sudden happiness filled her as she realized that Jack and Annie had come to the scene of the disaster together. Now, I know June enough to realize that she assumed that they shacked up together the night before, and the thought made her very happy indeed.

After seeing the devastation firsthand, Jack probably was a glutton for punishment because his next destination was the SharkFin, which was having a few problems of its own.

"Vandalism," I said flatly, standing behind my beloved bar which was in a state of disarray.

"I don't understand," Annie said, looking around the joint and seeing tables and chairs flung willy-nilly, broken bottles of booze, and the blue-lighted Christmas tree knocked on its side.

"Are you sure it wasn't a bear?" Jack asked.

"Don't get funny with me." I hadn't talked down to Jack in some years, but to be honest, I didn't like his tone on that morning. It was no time to crack jokes. My beloved tavern was ruined.

"How did they get in?" Annie asked.

"I closed the place early yesterday, in preparation for the storm. I'm thinking that's when they came in. There was practically no one downtown."

"But why?" Annie couldn't comprehend how something so horrible could happen in cozy Newport.

"It happens all the time during catastrophes." Jack sounded like an expert. "People lose their heads."

"Have you called the police?" Annie asked.

"They were already here." I leaned my elbows against the bar. "They took all the food from the fridge. When I called Josephine, she nearly wept. There was a good bag of fresh shrimp in there."

"Maybe they were homeless, hungry," Jack suggested.

"Twisted, deranged." Annie was fuming, and honestly, it made me feel proud. She was on my team. That's what crisis situations do; they let you know who's playing for your team.

Jack sighed, hands on hips. "I'll come clean it up tomorrow."

"You don't have to solve all the world's problems." Jack always liked to play the hero, and if you ask me, he sometimes spread himself too thin.

"Don't patronize me, Dad."

Silence followed as Annie's eyes went wide. It was the first time that she'd heard Jack call me dad before, and she must've found it shocking. Jack, as well, was taken aback, probably in shock that it had come from his mouth.

"I'm just saying, Tony," he went on, amending the situation. "If I want to be of help then you should just let me."

"Fine. I mean...yes. I'll let you."

Funny, the tense relations between father and son. God, I loved that kid so much, yet still, why was it sometimes hard to be open with him, and kind? I was protecting myself, that much in retrospect I know. There was so much that I felt guilty about and so much pain that I wished to take back.

"We should go." Jack walked towards the door.

Did I forget to mention how blissfully happy I was that Annie showed up to the SharkFin with Jack? It was the same elation that June felt, but times ten.

Annie put a loving hand on my shoulder. "I'm going to come by tomorrow to help, too,"

"They stole all the whiskey."

"I'll come anyway," Annie said with a lovely smile. She looked like an angel. It broke my heart.

But my heart revived when I watched the two of them leave the SharkFin together. I wish it could've been hand-in-hand, but that's life. One step at a time.

"You wanna get something to eat?" Jack asked as they walked back to his truck, bundled up against the cold. "You must be starving."

"I could use something, yeah." Annie heard concern and caring in his voice. Knowing Annie, I'm sure she questioned it, not thinking herself worthy. Such nonsense.

Just then, that familiar buzz was heard in Annie's bag, and her heart skipped a beat.

I don't want to freak you out, but the texts looked something like this:

Annie

Annie

Annie

Annie

Annie

Annie

WTF?

"What's wrong?" Jack asked, picking up on Annie's fear.

"It's nothing."

"It doesn't seem like nothing. You're shaking." Jack grabbed onto her elbow.

"It's cold."

Just then, the phone went off again and Annie couldn't hold onto the secret much longer. She remembered what I had told her earlier, and she acted accordingly.

"I'm getting a lot of texts…from Rory." Annie finally took out her phone and looked at the latest barrage.

Jack wanted to pull the phone from her hands and check himself, but he was going to be a gentleman about it. "What kind?"

"He's just very…insistent." Annie tried to explain it nicely. Luckily, Jack was no fool. He knew about Rory and his tendencies.

"He's scaring you."

"He's just…" Annie faltered.

"Scaring you. I can see it in your eyes." Jack studied Annie's eyes like a detective.

Annie was slightly unnerved that Jack was being so protective. "I don't need a knight in shining armor."

"Thank God, 'cause I'm not one." Jack opened Annie's car door.

That was a fucking lie. Pardon the language. He intended to be just that.

And so, that very afternoon, as Jack took Annie out to a waterside cafe, and her phone continued to beep and beep, Jack wasn't going to accept it for much longer.

"Annie, would you mind if I took your phone?" Half his burger still sitting in front of him.

"What?"

"Your phone," he repeated. "I'd like to talk to Rory."

Now, Annie wasn't the kind of lady that depended upon the kindness of strangers – well, Jack wasn't a stranger, but it's just an expression – but she had to admit that she was at the end of her rope.

She handed it over. "I feel uncomfortable about this."

"This just can't keep going on." Jack took it from her. He tapped on Rory's number and brought the phone to his ear. "Hey, it's Jack."

Now, Annie's heart was positively pounding in her chest. Needless to say, the Cobb salad in front of her wasn't going to be eaten.

"I think this has gone too far," Jack said into the phone as Annie wrung her napkin in her hands. "Just back off, man. You're making her uncomfortable."

The conversation was tame at first, but it wasn't long before things escalated. I can explain it to you in detail because it's now the stuff of Newport legend, but Rory asked to meet Jack in person so that they could discuss things, and Jack thought that was perhaps a good, gentlemanly way of handling it.

Of course, Annie wanted to have nothing to do with it, so she allowed Jack to drive her back to her apartment where she waited in dread to see what was going to happen. Jack dutifully met Rory at the SharkFin for a friendly beer where he'd express his concern in no uncertain terms.

At that point, if you'll recall, the SharkFin was still a mess, but I was there doing my best to clean it up. I still had some beer behind the bar – the vandals had taken the hard stuff – so I was more than happy to serve them what they required.

But let me tell you, the tension in that bar as those old friends sat there was like nothing I've ever experienced. I would have brought them out some chowder, just to ease the pressure – soup has the power to do that – but there was none. So alas, the boys went at it.

Now, I suppose that it was a good thing that the SharkFin already looked like a tornado went through it 'cause the guys went head-to-head. Of course, they sipped their beers first, discussed the matter at hand, but it was Rory who wasn't going to remain calm any longer.

"You always do this, Jack."

"Do what?"

"Step on my turf."

"Aren't we too old to be digging up all this old stuff?" Jack sensed where the conversation was going.

"You mean Lily? You're referring to Lily as old stuff?" Rory asked, clearly offended.

"Why don't we just stop this?"

"Why should we stop this?" Rory stood, hovering over Jack. "Why can't you admit that this is your fault? All of it? You're a greedy son of a bitch and you have been since we were kids."

I stepped back from the bar because I knew what was coming next.

Rory threw the first punch and Jack quickly ducked away from it. But if he was going to have to lay Rory down, then he'd do so. All that anger and blame for all of those years bubbled over and Jack pounced, similar to the way he had that first night when Annie was being pestered.

After a few quick punches, Rory was down and having a hard time getting up, and Jack wasn't going to push it any further. He'd made his message clear and that was that.

Let me be clear here that I'm not endorsing that kind of thing. There is that tendency in men, particularly when women and pride are involved, to need to physically express their aggression. Hell, a great deal of history is made up of just that. But the fight was short and sweet and I think that, in those few punches, Rory got the message loud and clear; don't blame Jack anymore.

Jack left the SharkFin as soon as we had Rory propped up on a bench with an icepack in his hand. He was done with Rory. I wish that I could tell you those friends would be able to patch it up with time, but sadly, that was not the case.

And so, Jack had the inclination to return to Annie, to tell her what happened and assure her everything would be alright. But instead, he needed to be alone, to process everything that had occurred, past, present, and future. I had to tell Annie myself about the beating that Rory got. And she soon discovered, in the days and weeks that followed, she wasn't bugged anymore by Rory. In fact, that kid left on his boat and never returned.

Chapter 18

The following day, Jack picked Annie up to take her to the lighthouse, as was promised. He preferred to take her at night so that they could turn back towards Newport and see the glittering lights from the lighthouse's vantage point. Annie wore her purple jacket to protect her from the cold, but Jack brought an extra blanket just in case.

"You ready for this?" he asked when she opened the door to her apartment.

"I'm excited."

She wasn't tentative about seeing the lighthouse. She actually was excited about that, but Annie didn't know how to feel about the fact that I had to be the one to inform her what happened between Jack and Rory. Annie could already understand that Jack was a fellow with a lot of pride, so maybe he found it embarrassing that he beat up an old friend in Annie's honor? At least that was what she assumed.

In truth, the fight with Rory, if discussed, would bring up another important conversation which Jack was not ready to talk about. At least, he didn't think so.

"Are we even allowed to be here?" Annie asked as they pulled up to the majestic lighthouse, the aerobeacon spinning its illuminated dance.

"I'm allowed to." Jack parked the truck and walked around to open Annie's door. "I know a guy." He smiled, taking her hand and helping her down.

"It's beautiful. I can see that light from my place at night." Annie felt the warmth of Jack's hand in her own.

"I can, too. I used to come up here a lot, when I was a kid."

"Oh?"

"Yeah, like I said, I know a guy." He grinned. "When things were tense at home, I'd come up here and just look out at the sea, enjoying the quiet."

"The lighthouse keeper let you do that?"

"Yes. Old Morris. He used to live here. Of course, there's no keeper now. It's just managed by local officials. I know those guys, as well."

"You've got friends in high places."

"I guess you could say that." Jack threw open the door to the lighthouse.

What was inside surprised Annie. She was expecting wet, dank walls, dead pigeons, old seashells, that sort of thing. But the inside of the lighthouse was warm and cozy, the walls dry and insulated, and the area expansive.

"When Morris was here there was furniture and whatnot, but they took it all out when he died."

"When was that?"

"About ten years ago."

"How did he die?"

"Old age, I think. Morris was nearing 100 years old."

"Wow." Annie was thinking about how it must've been to be an old fella like that, living alone in a lighthouse.

I'll tell you something, I knew Morris myself. He used to come into the SharkFin every year on his birthday and enjoyed a pint. He was always smiling. Morris was one of the happiest guys I've ever met. Unlike Hank, whom I see almost every day, who is a schmuck.

"Come on, let me take you upstairs." Jack was as excited as a kid. The lighthouse always had that effect on him. It was like he was transported in time.

Walking up the tight, windy stairs, Jack took Annie's hand once more to guide her. Of course, he didn't need to do that. She was a grown, capable woman who could walk upstairs by herself. But Jack was looking for any excuse to touch her. I'm just being honest here.

"Here we are." Jack was beaming with pride.

Annie took in the 360° view. "I can see my apartment!"

"There's Leavenworth." Jack pointed so that Annie could see. As he did so, he drew his cheek rather close to hers. It sent electricity up and down Annie's spine. Just trust me on this.

"Are you making progress?" Annie asked.

"You know, when my boat got stranded here, I was reluctant to get to work on it. But now that I'm in the flow of things, I think I'll have an unveiling soon."

"Are you serious?"

"Yes. I've been working day and night. You saw, over New Year's."

"Yes."

And mentioning New Year's was opening a huge can of warms, because Jack and Annie found themselves locked in one another's eyes for some time, reminiscing about the kiss, and mostly desiring to go in for another.

Jack held off, not wanting the lady to think that the only reason for having her there was to plant another one on her lips. Annie, as well, held back, not wanting Jack to think she was merely rewarding her knight in shining armor.

So, essentially, they were both thinking too much.

But it was perfectly fine that they held back because they enjoyed the silence for some time, looking out over Newport, blanketed in white, out towards the sea, laughing and telling stories. When Annie appeared a little cold, Jack ran back down to the truck and got the blanket that he knew would come in handy.

When he returned, he was surprised to find that Annie was no longer up in the tower, but had come back down to the main portion of the house.

"Is everything okay?" Jack asked, wondering if she got spooked while he was gone.

"I was just looking for some water." Annie didn't want to admit that she indeed got spooked when Jack was gone. She was thinking of the ghost of dead Morris.

"There's a faucet over here." Jack headed towards it but Annie stopped him, grabbing him by the hand. Jack was confused at first – blanket in his other hand – but then he got the message loud and clear when Annie drew in close and brought her lips to his.

Now, I'm not going to go into too much detail here, but the kiss was long and passionate, the blanket was eventually rolled out, and Jack and Annie found themselves lying on it, entangled around one another. You get the hint.

When the sun came up the following morning and Jack and Annie still found themselves in one another's arms, there was no talk of coffee or breakfast, no mad rush to get home. They enjoyed each other's company in much the same way, for the better part of the morning.

When Annie returned to her apartment that afternoon, she was on Cloud 9. I hate to be trite, but Jack was rocking her world, if you know what I mean. But seriously, she had never met someone so good, so genuine, and so 'all about her,' without any games being played, or strange artifice. Let's just say, when Annie arrived in Newport, she was nursing a broken heart – from the douchebag – and now she was finally letting go of the past, because the present was so much more interesting.

That day, she'd received a phone call from June, and she couldn't believe her ears.

"I need you to come downtown immediately."

"What's wrong?" Annie asked, thinking that she couldn't possibly handle any more bad news after what had happened to Newport Hollows.

"Nothing's wrong. Just excitement, Annie. I want you to be here to witness it."

"Okay, I can be there in 15 minutes or so."

"Perfect." Annie could almost hear June smile on the other end of the line.

"Where will I find you?"

"Main Street."

You'd think with a major blizzard just two days earlier, the roads would be a nightmare. But not in Newport. The volunteer firefighters had been working day and night to clear the roads.

Driving down Main Street and feeling proud that she was driving in the right direction, Annie spotted June immediately, because she was wearing a canary yellow coat the size of a sleeping bag while waving her hands wildly.

Not only was the smile on June's face a surprise, but also the change in hair color. June dyed it red, and later she would explain that it was Henna from the health food store.

"What is it?" Annie rolled down her window.

"Come on in here, you gotta see this."

Annie parked her car and did what she was told, entering a tiny little space with snow damage of its own to boast of.

"Are you moving in?" Annie asked humorously.

"Kind of." June threw her hands into the air. "I'd like to introduce you to the future Newport Flower Shop." Her face was beaming.

"Are you joking?" Annie was thinking the place looked more like a torture chamber.

"Used to be the old barber shop. It's been in disrepair for some time, but I'm going to transform it. Everywhere you turn there will be flowers, and fountains, and birds. Fake ones, of course. The birds."

"But June, doesn't this seem a little too soon?" Annie considered that the B&B was only recently destroyed.

"When one baby dies, it's best to make another one," June said, then realized just how macabre that statement really was. She sought to amend it. "I mean, I see what happened to Newport Hollows as an opportunity. I'll rebuild, of course, but it's going to take time. In the meantime, might as well embrace my dream."

"Oh, June. That's a wonderful way to look at it."

"We're going to sell the most beautiful flowers, and all year long. It'll be the light, life, and color that Newport really needs."

Annie wanted to tell June that she was all the light, life, and color that any town could possibly need. But she didn't.

"June, it's wonderful." Annie looked around at the sad storefront that had just been waiting for someone to revive it.

"With tragedy comes rebirth." June sighed to herself. Annie placed an arm around June's shoulder as it occurred to her that she'd be pretty darn lucky to have someone with June's spirit in her life for the rest of her days.

"You'll need a website. I'll write it for you."

"But you always say you hate writing for those websites. And why the heck would I need one for after all? To describe the flowers?"

"To describe the flowers, and to talk about you, why you started the business."

"I see." June considered it. "Well, I won't let you do it. You need all your spare time to work on your book."

"It's getting there."

"You haven't told me, is it a love story or a tragedy?"

"It's a love story," Annie said with a smile.

Just then, June finally could put her finger on why it was that Annie was glowing so much that afternoon. She knew the reason, without even asking, and it made her as happy as could be.

"That good, huh?" June asked with a twinkle in her eye. "What?"

"Never mind." June gave a knowing smile.

"I suppose that you heard about Rory." Annie thought that perhaps everyone in town already knew.

"Tony told me."

"I feel…embarrassed about the whole thing."

"Don't be. Rory had it coming, and those boys were meaning to duke it out for years."

"Still, I wish I had nothing to do with it."

"You were the catalyst, sure. But from what I understand, it's a situation that you won't worry about much longer."

"It's a relief when I think about it."

"Can I say something that you're not going to like? And then I'll buy you a muffin at Barringer's."

"Anything for a muffin from Barringer's."

"Can you let Jack take care of you? I know that he wants to."

Annie went silent as she considered June's words. What was it, the 1950s? Annie didn't fall for that kind of crap. And yet still, something deep down told her that maybe, just maybe, Jack was a man that she could trust.

Chapter 19

While so much was happening in Annie's life – the new apartment, car, romance, etc. – there was a secret life taking place, as well. A life that had more than a little to do with her actual life.

Don't get confused, I'm going to explain this to you. Now, I don't know a thing about writing or what it's like to be a writer. They always seem kinda tortured to me, and I can't type to save my life. I use my two pointer fingers. But what I know about Annie is that that thread of a secret life was always going on below the surface, and the thread became effortless and more golden while she was in Newport.

The story about the lady that goes to Paris was basically Annie's inner self. It was a woman that was starting over, letting go of the past, and finally seeing beauty around her in a way that she had forgotten was possible. Not only could Annie imagine the character in the book, she could feel her, within herself.

So, she was writing a ton each day. Annie told me her ritual once: get out of bed, make coffee, visualize that day, and then just start to write at a nice desk she had situated at the window, looking out over the water. She'd become enveloped in the world that she was creating. Entranced. And she didn't appreciate distractions.

And so, a good solid week after the storm, Annie found that she was mere weeks away from completing the story. The heroine had already left her old life, moved to Paris, started fresh, and was taking up painting. There was a love interest of course – just another element to the story that mirrored Annie's own life – but she hadn't yet decided how that love was going to end. Would it end in loss? Would they live happily ever after? Or like life itself, would it be something much more complicated? Something that fell in the middle.

That was the only aspect of the story that terrified her. She was stepping into the abyss, in her own life, and in her private world. The unknown is a funny thing, if you ask me. All of us are afraid of it, but I often like to think of the potential of things, you know. Why does everything have to be so scary?

Okay, I'm rambling.

Luckily for me, Annie found herself at the SharkFin to have a bit of lunch. There was a light crowd that afternoon, but of course, Hank was already in his cups.

"Annie!" Hank said, lifting up his beer to salute her as she came through the door. His words were a little slurred, but I knew Hank well enough at that point that he could recite Shakespeare entirely drunk and I'd understand everything that he was saying. Essentially, I spoke the language of drunk Hank.

"Hey, Hank." Annie seated herself at the bar. She wasn't there to drink, just to talk.

"You look happy," I said to her, leaning my elbow on the bar.

"Got a lot of work done today."

Indeed, there was something contented about her. It was that glowing look that one gets when they're either in love, creativity is flowing through them, or both. In Annie's case, it was definitely both.

"What are you having?" I asked.

There was obviously no need for Annie to look at the menu at that point.

"Fish and chips."

"Going big." It was like music to my ears.

"I actually find that I have quite the appetite today."

"Josephine will be thrilled."

Now, I don't want to get your mouth watering too much, but the fish and chips at the SharkFin comes in a family-sized portion. I mean, literally, it's one entire fried fish on a bed of French fries that could feed a football team. When I brought it out, Annie shook her head in dismay, laughing.

"You're going to help me with this, right?"

I looked from side to side, making sure that all my customers were taken care of, and relented.

"I don't require much encouragement." I grabbed a bottle of Heinz ketchup and made a nice puddle of it at the corner of the plate.

"I'm feeling nervous." Annie took a big bite of fish. She used her fork and knife to cut it off, which I was disappointed by. Fish and chips should be eaten with your hands.

"You don't look nervous," I said, taking a bite of five French fries at once.

"Well, I don't when I'm working, you know. It's just when I'm idle."

"What do you mean?" Although, I guess I knew what she was saying. When I was hard at work at the SharkFin, I was focused. Often when I got home, I would feel a little at a loss.

"The book will be done soon. Then what?" she asked.

"Then you publish it and become famous." Really, there was no other option to consider.

"It's not that easy, Tony. And I don't need to be famous. I just want people to enjoy it."

"Of course, people will enjoy it. The Book Club will fawn over it."

"I guess what I'm trying to say is, I don't know the ending." Annie put down her cutlery and considered what she just uttered.

"Of the book?"

"Of the book, yes. But also," she went on, and I leaned it, trying to see into that secret world of Annie. Unfortunately, it was more obscure than I wanted it to be. "The end of my story, you know. Moving here, making this big change, diving in. I don't know what's going to happen next."

"Annie." I dished out yet another pearl of wisdom. "Why do you want to know the ending when this is just the beginning?"

She sat and thought about it and took another bite of fish. It sounded trite, but I really did think it was a beginning for Annie, and not an ending.

Speaking of new beginnings, June was embracing her future with vigor. She learned from the contractor that

Newport Hollows was going to take months to rebuild, and in the meantime, since that was an undertaking that she had very little control over, she was diving head-first into her flower shop.

In fact, when Annie came to look at the place, more than midway through January, her jaw nearly dropped to the floor.

"June, how did you do it?" Annie asked, thinking that the shop was hardly recognizable from the first time that she saw it.

"It's still coming together." June walked past a display of white and purple irises. "But with time, I think it's going to be marvelous."

"It's already marvelous, June. I'm in shock."

"Why should you be in shock? You've tasted my pancakes, so you know that I can do anything."

The ladies shared a laugh and Annie breathed in the glorious aroma of exotic and not-so-exotic flowers. The irises were impressive, of course, but then there was the glass cooler displaying roses in every color of the rainbow. A little fountain was in the middle of the room, and it sported the statue of David, complete in all his naked glory. Of course, the first time I walked in there I had to turn away, but the ladies liked it.

What Annie found most impressive, and I have to admit that I preferred this as well, was the cactus wall. Considering June's love of Arizona, and still harboring dreams of retiring there, or at least buying a winter home, there was nothing more fitting than those remarkable cactuses both large and small, some flowering. Yes, I bought one of those cacti eventually, and I'll tell you why.

172

I have a black thumb. Can't keep a plant alive in my shack. So, essentially, the cactus was fitting.

"I want to sell chocolates, too. Right at the counter. That way, folks can buy a little something sweet for the ride home."

"Where will you get them from?" Annie asked.

"I'm going to make them, of course. Ever since Newport Hollows bit the dust, I feel idle without cooking for people. Like I'm not myself anymore."

"Oh, you're still yourself, I promise you." Annie looked down at June's sky-blue blouse. The shell necklace was still worn diligently.

"How is the romance department?" June asked, fiddling with some hydrangeas.

"Oh, stop." Annie waved her hand in the air.

"Come on. It's not like no one knows. You're positively glowing, and what's more, I hear that Jack has transformed Leavenworth in the way he always dreamed. Seems like something is driving all this positive energy, huh?" June winked at Annie.

"We are enjoying our time together."

That was an understatement, let me tell you. When those two were together, they beamed. Life had hope and purpose, as it always does when one is in love. And I can tell you in no uncertain terms that those kids were in love.

"You see the house?" June was dying to host an unveiling of Leavenworth so the whole community could come and enjoy Jack's hard work.

"He won't let me see it," Annie protested.

"What do you mean?"

"Not since New Year's. He says that he wants it to be a surprise."

"Well, that's rather sweet of him." June leaned on the shop's counter. "He really cares about you."

"We have fun dinners at my place. I can't cook, of course, but we order out, watch movies, just sit and chat. He's a really decent man."

"You can say that again."

"But there's still something, uh," Annie was choosing her words carefully, "*impenetrable* about him. I know that a lot has happened in his past."

"A lot that hasn't been reckoned with." June lifted her brows.

"What do you mean?"

"I mean, it's never been patched up between Tony and Jack. No discussion of the past. It's like everything that's happened to them in this town is just a ghostly memory, haunting them wherever they go."

So, here in the telling of the story, I have to be a little delicate because I'm a key player. But what June said was true. Jack and I learned to move on with our separate lives, not getting in each other's way. Every so often, he'd come into the SharkFin, and that was that. I had to hear about his life from others.

"You know, sometimes people just need to duke it out," June said. "Bring up the old crap and put it to rest."

It was mildly insensitive of June to say so, but I'll concede that she had a point. Annie, on the other hand, was not convinced.

"Like Jack and Rory did?"

June nodded her head. "Precisely."

174

"I'm not so sure that aggression of any sort is the answer."

"I'm not saying they gotta throw punches, but sometimes a bit of emotional aggression is required to unearth what the hell is bugging you."

"Aggression?"

"Annie, I'm going to tell you something now that has helped me in the past." June embraced her teaching moment. She had been through nearly as much as I'd been through in my life, and I have to admit that she handled it better, so the advice was sound. "We become sad and hopeless when we aren't forward-footed in our lives, you know? You gotta be aggressive with what you want, letting go of the past, fighting for your own heart. Yes, I'm saying that sometimes you should fight, but it doesn't have to be with your firsts. You just tell the universe loud and clear where you're coming from, and where the heck you want to go. Yell it if you have to."

Annie smiled. It was the best advice she'd heard in some time.

Chapter 20

And speaking of the courage to face the past, that topic suddenly came to mind, and all because of Annie's doing. She had invited me for coffee at Barringer's; had something to talk about. Now, my mind was reeling. I was thinking, she's informing me that she and Jack are getting married, having babies, all that wonderful stuff that Jack would never tell me. Unfortunately, that was not so.

"Do you and Jack ever talk?" she asked, and I was stunned that she was pushing the subject. I ordered a cheese Danish and took a nervous bite of it in response. Felt the crumbs fall on my chin, which I wiped away with my hand.

"You're not making this date very romantic."

"I don't mean to barge into your business, Tony. It's just that, I can feel the tension, and you're my friend."

"There's some tension, yes."

"Maybe if you guys talked it out, you could work through some stuff."

Annie had ordered the famous blueberry muffin which she cut in half with a knife. That wasn't very ambitious, in my opinion.

"Listen, I've tried to talk to Jack. I've been trying for a while. He makes it very clear that he doesn't want to have the discussion."

"Well, it's clear that you're going to have to initiate it, because Jack won't. I know that well enough."

So, she knew Jack well at that point? Of course, she did, because she was in love. But with love came blinders, and I don't think that Annie yet realized how much Jack didn't like to talk about things.

"Have you had this conversation with him?" I asked, not defensively, I promise you.

"No. I guess I've been afraid to."

"Don't be afraid of Jack. He won't bite."

"I don't know. I've seen him take a guy down to the floor. Heard about another guy that he did the same to. All while in your bar." Annie spoke humorously, although I knew that the situation with Rory had really pained her.

"Annie, can I ask you something?"

"Of course."

"Why you asking me to do this? I mean, we're close now, right?"

"We are."

"So, why has this come up? I'm curious."

"I just want to see you and Jack happy."

What I think she wanted to say was that she saw a future with Jack, and it would warm her heart if he could let go of the past and move forward. With her.

"Well, I'm going to think about all this." I took another bite of the Danish.

"Please, don't just think about it, but really consider taking action. Being courageous."

"Courageous, huh?"

Annie had a real point. There was so much of my past that I hadn't contended with, didn't want to look at. So much had gone wrong, and in my life, I ended up in a very different place than I wanted to end up. Don't get me wrong, I loved working at the SharkFin, loved living in the shack, but I gotta admit that I saw it all going a whole lot differently back in the day.

For one thing, I imagined that Elizabeth would still be alive, we'd be living at Leavenworth, I'd be a man of luxury, maybe with a desk job. I also thought that Jack was going to be my loving son. But none of that happened. Life took me for a real funny ride. The drinking didn't help. It was just the nail in the coffin that was already prepared to lay itself in the ground.

Okay, I'm getting real dark on you.

After coffee, I went to my post behind the bar and had a typical day. Served Hank about 300 drinks, poured soup for the tourists, and made it to the eleventh hour when everyone straggled out and I was left with the cleanup. Gregor was there. Remember Russian Gregor? He'd been absent from our story for a while. Mostly, he wished to talk about Jack.

"Got to get that man back on the boat very soon," Gregor said, shaking his head.

"He's going to be in Newport a lot longer than you think." I winked, Annie still on my mind.

"I beg to differ." Gregor lifted his glass of beer into the air. "Fair weather is coming our way. You can't keep Jack out of the sea for very long."

It was his mediocre English. You can't keep Jack *off* of the sea for very long. Sadly, it was a statement that I'd end up thinking about for a long time to come.

I got Gregor mildly drunk so that he'd stop talking about Jack going away, and then he and Hank were the last two to go.

By the way, I forgot to tell you, the SharkFin cleaned up nicely, and I even put the blue Christmas tree back up in defiance of those stupid vandals. The cops hadn't even caught them yet.

So, I leaned upon the bar and looked at the tree, marveling at how, when things fall apart, they seemed to come together in their own time. The time for rebuilding depended upon the severity of the destruction.

What happened next you can fully trust me on, because I was there. It was after the conversation with Annie that I called Jack up from the phone behind the bar. Yes, the SharkFin still had a real phone attached to the wall.

"Hey, kid." I instantly regretted it. I loved calling Jack kid, like I did when he was a boy, but I don't think he appreciated it much.

"Hey, what's up?" His tone placid.

"Can you come by here tomorrow night?"

"What for?"

I tried to sound casual. "Just wanted to catch up with you, that's all."

There was silence after that as Jack considered my invitation.

"What time?"

"I dunno. Maybe 7?"

"Yeah sure," Jack replied. "Listen, Tony, I gotta go."

"Okay. I'll see you tomorrow."

"Fine."

I don't know why he agreed to it. Maybe Annie had already told him about our conversation regarding the issue, or perhaps there was something within himself, as well, which knew that it was time to face things. The standoff had gone on for too long, and it wasn't helping anyone.

As the next day rolled around, I closed the SharkFin early. Barely any customers anyhow. There was a blustery wind outside and pelting rain, which was a bad sign in terms of icy roads. But Jack braved the storm, as he always did, and drove in his truck. I knew he arrived when the bright headlights poured through the SharkFin's windows and directly to where I stood behind the bar.

"Jesus." I brought my hand up to shield my eyes. "What an entrance."

And that wasn't the half of it either. Jack flung open the door, wearing a nautical parka, totally dripping with water. It kinda reminded me of that first night when I saw Annie, practically pushed through the door on the wind.

"Nasty out there." Jack closed the door behind him and shook off the water.

"Tomorrow is going to be a hell of a morning. We could go ice skating down Main Street," I joked, trying to begin by lightening things up.

"I guess."

He plopped himself down on the stool and looked around the joint.

"Slow night?"

"I closed the place early."

"Oh, then this is serious." Jack wasn't making eye contact with me.

"You want a beer?"

"I'm fine, thanks."

"Okay, well. Thank you for coming. I just figured…it's been a long time since we had a good chat."

Jack finally looked into my eyes. "Are you dying?"

"No, but I appreciate your concern," I replied, noting that Jack didn't sound concerned at all.

"Then what is this about?"

"I just thought that maybe we should talk. Clear some things up."

I wanted to throw Annie under the bus just then, tell Jack that this was all her doing and that he shouldn't blame me, but that would be cowardly and unfair to Annie, in my estimation.

"What would you like to clear up?" Jack's tone became serious. "And yes, I'll take that beer now."

I poured him a Guinness, took a deep breath, and dove right in.

"I need to apologize to you kid." Shit, shit, shit.

"Okay, so you just apologized."

"Don't be cold with me." I didn't that he couldn't drop his facade.

"You apologized. Thank you. What more do you want?"

"I want you to forgive me."

It was a simple statement, but it was the truth. I'd been waiting in silent desperation for years to receive Jack's forgiveness.

Jack ran a hand through his hair. "Jesus, Tony."

"I'm your father. You don't have to call me Tony."

"You want me to forgive you for abandoning me when I needed you most, huh? Mom dies, my world falls apart, and when I need you to be a man and step up, you become a drunk. You abandoned me, you abandoned Leavenworth, and your own goddamn self."

I spoke softly. "Yes, all of this is true." It hurt like bloody hell to hear him say it, but it was all the truth.

"And then, I need you again after Lily dies. Hell, I needed anyone, even your drunk version, but you were a fucking ghost."

"I was ashamed of myself, Jack."

"You had every goddamn right to be. And you still do today. And you ask for my forgiveness? I'll forgive you when you're dead."

"You'll forgive me when you have a family of your own."

Jack looked up from his beer, his eyes becoming soft and misty. I couldn't tell if he thought my statement was true or just pathetic on my part. But I did sense that it would be so. Jack would have a family, and then he'd finally see how hard it was. How you never felt good enough as a parent, and a spouse.

"I know I lost control." I spoke through the tense silence, the only other thing audible was the pouring rain outside the SharkFin's windows. "I just wish you could understand –"

"How painful it is to see someone that you love and protect die on you? How, as a man, that makes you feel helpless, useless? You don't think I understand that, Tony?" Jack stood from the bar stool. He towered over me, that kid.

I found him physically intimidating, which was humbling as a father. "Did I become a drunk when Lily died?"

"That's not fair."

"That's not fair? How is that not fair? You had responsibilities to me, to mom, to this town. You let yourself go, and I think that you relinquished the right to have anyone forgive you." Jack reached in his pockets and threw a five-dollar bill down on the bar. "Thanks for the talk."

I watched as he walked out of the SharkFin.

I'd like to say that I was a tough guy at that point, but you know me better than that by now. I placed my head in my hands and cried. Could still hear the rain outside.

Chapter 21

The next installment of the book club was momentous, indeed. Not only was it taking place in June's flower shop, it was also a time for members to read the better portion of Annie's almost-finished book.

It was like having a club meeting in a tight-packed rainforest. The flower shop was humid, in order to cater to the more exotic flowers, while those that needed a little cooling were in the fridge. Consider what it was like to have a bunch of post-menopausal biddies in one tightly-cramped space, and you'll get the picture. Aluminum chairs were arranged in a circle.

"I need lemonade," Peggy said, fanning herself.

"I need a vodka and tonic," Myrtle added.

"Now, now, ladies. This humidity is good for the skin, especially in this dry winter wonderland." June passed out copies of the book club newsletter. There was a calendar for the upcoming discussions, as well as who'd be bringing the snacks. Although June always liked to cater most meetings, she thought the ladies might enjoy bringing in their own creations, each dish themed towards the book that they were discussing that week.

To Gayle's dismay, she would need to bring refreshments for Love in the Time of Cholera.

Annie was nervous and wringing her hands. The ladies had received the manuscript a week before, so they'd have plenty of time to peruse it. But Annie feared that maybe they hadn't even tried, or worse, didn't like it at all. Even more disconcerting was the fact that Samantha was staring at her from behind her very serious eyeglasses.

June grinned. "Now, we have a very important book to discuss this week." She passed around a tray of macarons. "I'm sure you've all had a chance to read the pre-ordered, unnamed masterpiece that will soon be in bookstores around the county."

Annie muttered. "They get the point, June."

"Now, now, Annie, don't be shy. I'd like to know who is willing to open this discussion."

June looked around the cramped shop, Peggy continued to fan herself, and Samantha took out a bottle of red vitamin water.

"I would like to," Myrtle said gravely, raising her wrinkled hand in the air.

"Alright, Myrtle. Why don't you start us off?" June seated herself in her chair. She handed off the last tray of sliced baguette topped with brie and candied walnuts.

"Annie, we haven't known you for long, although it feels like it's been an eternity."

"Oh God," Annie said under her breath.

"I mean that in a good way." Myrtle smiled tightly. "We've been through a lot together, and all this while, we didn't know exactly what you were working on while you were settling into Newport."

185

"A masterpiece!" Peggy blurted out, causing Samantha to nearly spit out her vitamin water. Myrtle turned to Peggy and scowled.

"Will you let me finish for once? All that money and no manners."

"Speak, Myrtle." June wished to move past the drama and get to the important business at hand.

"Annie, this book is a gem," Myrtle finally said. It was like the temperature in the room changed. A cool wave of air moved through and everyone heaved a collective sigh of relief and pleasure. Yes, they all read the book, and they all loved it.

"I couldn't put it down." Samantha was unable to contain her words. "And when I got to the end, and realized that there really was no end, I felt faint."

"You should get checked for anemia," Gayle said like a worried school teacher.

"What I'm trying to say is, it's just so moving and original. It speaks to the heart of the disconnection and inner struggles of the modern woman. It's about wanting what we're supposed to want, then learning that what we thought we wanted wasn't what we wanted at all." Samantha straightened her glasses on her nose.

Myrtle spoke. "The character in the book; Amelia. She's in her thirties. But I have to say, this appeals to women of all ages. I really connected to Amelia."

"So, did I," Peggy interjected.

"I did, too," June added. "God bless her, she thought she could depend upon men. That they would make her happy and contented. She put up with all their bullshit and was left with nothing."

Peggy was in shock. "Well, I do think we can rely on men a little bit."

"If they're loaded," Myrtle whispered.

"I'm just saying," June went on. "It's about finding yourself, even if you have to travel across the world to do it."

All eyes turned towards Annie as the little crowd waited for her to speak. Women sitting in the back whispered to one another about god knows what. Women just like to whisper, I suppose.

Annie cringed. "Is it like *Eat, Pray, Love*?"

"Nooooooo!" the ladies collectively replied.

Not that there was anything wrong with that book. In fact, I'm told it's great. I think that Annie just wanted to make something original, deeper, more nuanced.

"How does it end?" Samantha asked. Annie could swear that she saw tears in the girl's eyes just thinking about it.

Taking a deep breath, Annie replied amidst the expectant silence.

"I don't know." She shrugged her shoulders towards her ears.

"You don't know?" The words were like poison in Myrtle's mouth.

Samantha tried to put the pieces together. "She's on the boat from Paris. With Henri. They're going to New Caledonia."

Myrtle picked it up. "Amelia's not sure if she can trust Henri, after getting the shit kicked out of her by men."

"Myrtle!" Peggy protested.

"Well, it's true."

Annie looked out the window. "Yes, she's on the boat to New Caledonia. Henri has made her promise to have an open mind about the future. But I don't know what awaits her there."

**

Sadly, a week later, Annie was still at a loss as to what happened to Amelia when she made it to New Caledonia. It was probably due to the fact that she was a little bit at a loss as to what was happening between her and Jack. He was still being affectionate, coming over for dinner, calling her during the day, being the gentleman. He always was, but something was a little off.

She had asked me about it, and obviously, I told her all about what happened between Jack and I at the SharkFin. It made Annie sad to hear, because she wanted resolution and no more fighting. But resolution was definitely not what was reached that night.

That being said, a certain kind of weight had been lifted. I had done my best to make it right, and I was denied. If I had to take that to my grave, then I would. I wasn't perfect, still ain't perfect, and I can tell you with some clarity that I never will be. But I did try to do my best.

So, Annie expressed those concerns to me regarding Jack and I became a little worried. If he was deciding to pull away from Annie, then I had misjudged his character all along.

I had a hunch as to what was *really* going on between those two, and within a few days' time, my theory would prove to be right.

Jack stood in Annie's apartment. "I'm taking you somewhere."

"Where?" Annie thought maybe they were going on a date, or back to the lighthouse. She would've been happy about that, because it was one of the most memorable nights of her life.

"I have to blindfold you." Jack had a guilty smile.

"So, it's that kind of date."

"Just trust me, okay?" Jack pulled out a piece of fabric from his pocket.

Annie obliged, put on the blindfold, and was led to Jack's truck. When she arrived at the passenger door, he picked her up and plopped her inside. She weighed practically nothing in his arms.

All throughout the drive, Annie kept giggling and asking questions, but Jack wouldn't bite. When they finally pulled up to their destination, Annie had a good idea where they might be because the drive was the distance from her place to Leavenworth.

When he pulled the blindfold down, Annie audibly gasped. The facade of Leavenworth was covered in beautiful white lights, the hedges were perfectly trimmed, and a fountain had been placed in the roundabout, bubbling and glistening with its own twinkly lights.

"Oh my God, Jack." Annie brought her hands to her cheeks.

"That's just the start of it."

Leading Annie inside, I know that Jack was brimming with pride, while also apprehensive about what she might think.

I'm not lying here when I tell you that Leavenworth had been redone in a fashion that could compete with The Breakers. Most of that was due to the huge amount of vintage crap that was downstairs in the basement, having finally been brought up and positioned just right. Not only that, Jack, and a team of guys, of course, had redone the interior, the wainscoting, molding, you name it. And that was just the hallway.

Bringing Annie to the main room overlooking the water, the same room where they enjoyed New Year's by each other's side, Annie felt as though she'd stepped into something out of a fairytale.

"Jack, I don't even know what to say."

"It needed to be done. I've just been away too much."

"It's pure magic. You're a magician!"

That brought a great smile to Jack's face.

"Come here." He took Annie into his arms and kissed her. Jack had a habit, when he was really happy, of stealing kisses from Annie. She learned that that was just par for the course, and she was game.

They finally came up for air.

"Is this why you've been...distant lately?"

"Distant?" Jack asked.

"I don't know. Something seemed a little off."

"Strange."

Okay, folks, let me explain something here. This phenomenon was not strange at all. It's commonly known that when a man is getting serious about a girl, he pulls back a little. A man's gotta think about things. So not only was he busy with the house, he was also busy worrying about what Annie would think of it, and more than that, he was thinking a lot about the future. Jack needed space for all that.

"When are you going to show it to the public?"

"Right now," Jack said, looking down at his watch.

"What?"

"Yep, June and the girls should be here in twenty minutes. She's bringing food and I bought the libations."

"Amazing." Annie was overjoyed.

"You know." Jack put his hands around Annie's waist. "You've been a little distant, too."

"I have?"

"Yeah, I mean. Something has seemed strange."

"Well, I guess I've just been busy with the book. The girls loved it, but I still can't figure out the ending."

It was then that, despite her embarrassment, Annie explained the character of Amelia on the boat with Henri, heading to New Caledonia. Jack thought it sounded pretty exotic, but he was intrigued by anything that was on Annie's mind.

"You don't know what happens to her?"

"No, not yet."

A fun idea came to Jack's mind, and a fine way to break the mild tension that they had felt.

"You free tomorrow?" Jack asked.

"Um...I think so."

"Good." He smiled at her mischievously.

Chapter 22

So, what happened next was like something out of a movie. Actually, the kind of movie that Annie liked to watch most.

Jack picked her up late morning and told Annie to bundle up. She grabbed her purple coat and off they went into Jack's truck, which ventured down towards the marina. There in the water, neglected for too long, was Jack's boat, the Spanish Princess. She swayed softly from side to side, enjoying the seemingly fair weather.

"Is this the same boat you rescued us on? That day with Rory?" Annie felt apprehensive even mentioning his name.

"Same boat." Jack hopped aboard and held out his hand to help Annie on.

"It's very nice." Annie examined it with fresh eyes. The first time that she was on it, there was far too much fear and panic for her to even see straight.

"It's functional. Fishing boasts aren't supposed to be beautiful. Well, I guess they have their own kind of beauty," Jack explained. "They are plain beauties. Nothing fancy."

For a moment, her heart sank. Annie always considered herself to be a plain beauty. Nothing fancy. It was something that she always contended with inside of herself. Should she be flashier? Womanlier? I could have told her flat-out that Jack wouldn't want that for a second. In fact, he wouldn't want Annie to change a hair on her head.

"Hold on," Jack said. "Make yourself cozy in here. I gotta grab something."

As Annie went down a ladder into the belly of the boat, she found that it really was cozy indeed down there. There was a dining table, a few beds for the other fishermen and Jack to sleep in, as well as a fridge and whatnot. What surprised her was how well-appointed it was. Again, nothing fancy, but fine American quilts, little vintage pictures on the walls, and a few plastic Tiffany lamps.

First let me explain that last bit. Jack always had a thing for those Tiffany lamps because he grew up seeing the real deal at Leavenworth. So, when he found some plastic ones at a novelty store, he snatched them right up. His reasoning was, when the Spanish Princess was in a tempest, those plastic lamps could withstand being tossed about a bit.

"It's not bad, huh?" Jack climbed down the ladder. He had a wicker basket in his hand.

"It's really nice."

"You're really nice." Jack put the basket down on the table, then came over to give Annie a kiss.

They finally went up to the cockpit, where Jack had already turned the heater on, and off they went. Annie liked to watch Jack when he was behind the captain's wheel. He drove the boat with incredible focus and assurance. All the while that he kept his eyes ahead, Annie sat on a little stool behind him as Jack explained the importance of safety, fisherman's etiquette, and a whole bunch of stuff that I don't understand. Annie, of course, was impressed, as ladies often are by that sort of thing. But Jack wasn't trying to be impressive.

"Can I ask you something?"

"Of course, you can," Jack replied, glancing back towards her.

"I mean, I've always wanted to be on your boat with you. But, is there a reason why you wanted to do this today? I mentioned the book last night…"

Jack grinned to himself like a mischievous boy, just as he had done the night before, and Annie cocked her head in wonder.

Without replying, Jack turned off the engine and dropped anchor. It was perfectly alright to do so since the waters were calm that day. As he ran around the boat making preparations, Annie looked out towards the grey sea and sighed to herself. For the first time in a while, the book wasn't on her mind, the shitty copywriting wasn't on her mind, or the riddle of her future. She was content.

"Come down here." Jack motioned towards the trapdoor into the lower room.

"Okay." Annie laughed to herself. She liked when Jack was mischievous. It looked good on him.

When she climbed down the ladder, Jack helping her all the way, she found yet another surprise. It was the second one in two days.

"Jack!" she exclaimed, seeing the Parisian picnic that had been laid out on the table.

"I don't know if it's accurate." Jack scratched his head.

"It's perfect." Annie placed her hand over her heart.

Sure enough, Jack did a little research on the subject. He had a baguette, which was crucial, three different kinds of cheese, charcuterie, grapes, mustard, and other kinds of spread, as well as a bottle of red wine. I would've told him to serve white in the afternoon, but if I did, Jack would just look at me confusedly.

As they sat down, Jack poured the wine and took two plates from the basket. They were actually fine china plates from Leavenworth, because Jack thought the occasion too important to bring paper.

They dug into the food and Annie was swooning. What was it about those faux Parisian picnic meals that was so satisfying? Basically, I think it was because humans really only need to live off bread and cheese.

"So, this is why you brought me here," Annie said with a smile.

"Well, you mentioned the book, and the boat. The lead character not knowing what happens next."

"Yes."

"I think she should end up with the guy." Jack put his hand out, grasping Annie's. "I think that they should have a future together. On the island."

Annie nearly choked on her wine.

Okay, so it wasn't a marriage proposal, but that was fine enough in Annie's estimation. She didn't need to get married. Wasn't even sure she wanted to. What she truly desired, deep down, was a future with Jack. And the reason why is because, if this makes any sense, Annie also wanted a future with herself. Jack was the kind of guy that would let her do that, always encourage her to be herself and to be her best, while still being by his side.

"Tony loves you, you know." Annie was unsure as to why it flew out of her mouth.

Jack pulled his hand away and sat back, unable to process what he was hearing.

"He has a funny way of showing it."

"I'm just saying. I don't want to pry. I just see the situation from both sides."

"So, he told you about the other night?"

"He did."

"Well, I guess I've been thinking about it a lot." Jack took a sip of his red wine. "I know that he's sorry and all that. He said as much."

"And he means it."

"I just don't know how to let him win."

Annie had to consider that statement for a moment. I'm glad she did, because I wouldn't have been too happy if I had heard it with my own ears.

"What do you mean, let him win?"

"I mean, that's what this is about, isn't it?" Jack was becoming indignant. "If I forgive him, then the past was nothing. Water off his back. He wins."

"I don't think that it works that way."

"Explain that."

"By forgiving him, you are the one that wins," Annie began to explain. "Don't you see how much of this you're carrying on your shoulders? How much of it still lives in you? I think that by forgiving him, you release that weight."

Although Jack didn't wish to continue the conversation, in the silence that followed, Annie's words really struck home. He'd been carrying that weight around. Could really feel it. Would he benefit by forgiving me?

Now, I have to be careful how I talk about all this because I wasn't there, of course. But Annie told me later

196

that she saw the change, and it happened pretty quickly. Jack softened. His heart opened up. And I'm sure glad that it did.

I received the phone call later that night. I was behind the bar and it was pretty busy if you ask me. Hearing Jack's voice on the other end, I ignored my customers and put the priority where it lay, with my son.

"Hey."

"Hey," I replied, thinking it was good manly verbiage to use when two guys were speaking after a huge fight.

"I was out on the boat with Annie today." A huge smile came to my lips. Even though it was a kind of diversion, I still liked the fact that Annie came up in the conversation.

"Was a nice day for it."

"Yeah."

Silence.

"Listen, Jack. I got a few customers." I thought that if the conversation was just going to be silence then there was no point to it.

"Just hear me out for a second."

"Alright."

"About our talk the other night. I'm sorry that I stormed out of there the way that I did."

"It's okay, kid. I understand."

"I have more to say."

"Right."

"Not only am I sorry that I stormed out, but I regret…" Jack's voice became hoarse and something in my chest constricted. He tried to continue, but it was still hard to get the words out. "I regret…not…forgiving you sooner."

I heard Jack crying on the other end of the line. Tears were welling in my own eyes, but I tried to push them back. There would be nothing worse than a middle-aged bartender losing his shit behind the bar, and during a busy shift. That being said, the SharkFin totally melted away in that moment. It was just me and Jack, my son, having the most important conversation of our lives.

"I only ask forgiveness, kid," I said through my tears. "You don't have to give it to me. I understand the hurt that I've done."

"You've always done your best, Dad. I know that you did your best."

"Okay." It was hard to speak. My chest was heaving.

"I'm gonna go."

"Okay."

Basically, Jack and I ended the conversation because neither of us could get any more words out. And quite frankly, there was nothing else that needed to be said. It was simple, to the point, and it healed the bond between us. Of course, it didn't heal the pain, the immense pain that could only come from unexplainable tragedy. But it did open a new bridge between us and for that I was eternally grateful.

Jack didn't tell Annie what he'd done, not immediately anyway. He stood on the balcony of Leavenworth, the balcony where his mother once stood, and looked out towards the water, allowing the cool air to wash over him.

There'd been a weight on Jack's shoulders for such a long time. It was always palpable to me. And I know, that night on the balcony, he finally let it go. There was a new life ahead of him. If you ask me, I think it's because Annie came into town. Funny how other people can veer us off course or steer us towards the shore.

Chapter 23

Something funny was in the air. Everyone in Newport could tell. It was one of those weird celestial occurrences where dogs start barking for no apparent reason. Doors randomly shut when no one else is in the room. The TV suddenly turns on when no one has the remote.

You can ask one of those New Age people about why this might be. They'd reply that it was something in the stars, or the way that the planets were aligning. Whatever might be the explanation, something was off.

It happened for a couple of days, and I felt it at the SharkFin. I took the tree down, which was already making me sad, so I decided to light candles on the bar to create a fun 'vibe,' as the kids call it. A little atmosphere, you know. So, I get all the candles lit, I'm waiting for Annie to walk through the door and tell me about the completion of her book, and just like that, all of those candles went out except for one. I scratched my head and went into the kitchen to tell Josephine.

"Is there a draft in here?"

She was slaving away over a pot of chowder, looking flummoxed.

"I don't feel a draft in here," Josephine replied, "I'm hot as hell." She fanned herself. Like the biddies at the book club, Josephine had temperature issues. "But I can tell you that this chowder is no good. It's got no flavor."

"Did you put in enough salt?" I walked over. Josephine took a ladle-full of soup and brought it to her mouth, taking a sip.

"There's enough salt in there to shame the Dead Sea." Josephine shook her head. She handed me the ladle so that I could give it a try. Tasting it, I saw that she had a point.

"You sure you got all the spices in there?"

She shot me a look that could cut diamonds.

Customers started to roll in and I relit the candles. That time, they stayed put for a while, until Annie walked through the door, and then they all went out again.

I poured her a whiskey. "You notice anything off about today?"

"Tony, I had the funniest thing happen to me. It's amazing that you asked."

"What was it?"

"This morning, I woke up at my normal time. I slept well," she began to explain, sitting on the stool and taking off her coat. "And when I reached over for my cell phone, it wasn't there."

Leave it to a quasi-millennial to think something is off in the world because they can't locate their phone. But there was more to the story.

"I get out of bed and walk over to the dresser, and sure enough, there it was, lying face down on the floor and completely smashed."

"You threw it across the room," I replied.

"I must have, but why?"

"It's a real mystery."

"Anyways. Yes, I guess that it is a weird day. It spooked me for some reason."

"Maybe it was a victory toss, like dropping the mic." I smiled, lifting my brow. "You're done, aren't you?"

"I am." Annie's face broke into a glorious smile.

"And how does it feel?"

"I have to admit, it's amazing. I can't believe the book is done."

"I'm sure it's a masterpiece, Annie."

"I think the thing that matters most is that it's done. I made it all the way through. And you know what, I think it's pretty good."

"Got your happy ending?"

"Yes. The ending is happy. It's very happy."

"You gonna celebrate with Jack?"

I had already told Annie about the fateful phone call, and she was over-the-moon when she heard the news. The bond between her and Jack only strengthened after that.

"I can't. He's leaving tomorrow morning."

"What do you mean he's leaving tomorrow morning?" I leaned my elbow on the bar.

"He's going out, for his first trip in a long time. He's heading to Maine."

"You sure that's a good idea?"

So, here's what I'll say at this juncture. I was worried about the storm that was coming in. All the reports were saying that it wasn't going to be so bad, but still, I had the thought that it was a terrible idea. That being said, what drove away those concerns was the intense happiness that I

202

felt that night. Candles or no candles, chowder or no chowder, Annie had completed her book, she was in love, and her life was moving forward in new and remarkable ways. It was everything that I wanted for her from the first moment that I met her. That night when she came into the SharkFin with eye liner streaming down her face and a broken heart, Annie had lost hope. And to my amazement – but not my surprise – Newport had restored all that.

"You wanna know what happens on New Caledonia, when Amelia and Henri get there?" Annie asked, mischief in her eyes.

"I most certainly do." I poured Annie her second whiskey. Heck, she was celebrating. I was drinking a ginger ale behind the bar.

"They fall in love, of course. Everyone already knew that. But it turns out that Henri has a little house there. A kind of fancy island cottage. Amelia decides to stay, and not return to Paris. They turn the cottage into a home and Annie and Henri get married. They have a child."

"That's a wonderful ending." I wanted to reach out and pinch Annie's cheek. Or kiss her on the forehead.

"Yes, I thought that was a good ending."

Things are going to take a turn here, friends, and for that I want to apologize, but things end up going down the course that they go. If I've learned anything in life, it's that you gotta let the river run in the direction it's going to run. And when it does so, if you need to cry like a child or scream like a banshee, then do it.

Jack went out on the water that next morning with high hopes. The smell of the sea filled his nostrils, and as he and Gregor, accompanied by two other men, went out to sea, they were joking and amiable as always. Hell, they were all excited. It had been too long since they made their last journey up the coast to Maine.

The storm took everyone by surprise. The weathermen would get the brunt of the blame. But what started as a big but benign storm turned into something much different, and I'm afraid that it took the crew of the Spanish Princess in its clutches.

What the reports would later determine was that there was some problem with the boat itself, damage from the long time at port. So, when the Spanish Princess malfunctioned, already well up the coast and out of reach, it came as quite a shock as the storm hit hard and unexpectedly fast.

The waves crashed violently, and Jack, always the one to remain calm, commanded the crew and did his best to keep an even head about him. When a particularly hard wave hit, it was Gregor that was flung overboard, and not wearing a life vest at that. It was custom for fishermen to put those vests on when a storm hit, but everything happened so fast that no one thought ahead.

The rain came in sideways, the waves were relentless, and Gregor was choking in the sea. Jack, without thinking, without pausing, dove in and swam like hell to grab Gregor. He knew that it would take much time before Gregor went under, and Jack was a strong enough swimmer to get him back to the ship in the time that was necessary.

It was dark out there on that sea. Jack didn't feel any fear, he only knew that he had a duty. All those men were under his command. So, as he swam intrepidly towards Gregor, there was no way that he could see that arrant piece of driftwood in the water. It would've been impossible for anyone to see. It rolled in on a wave and was pointed directly towards Jack's head. Nothing gruesome, I promise you, but Jack instantly was knocked out by it, and well...

Friends. I'm a little tongue-tied now, which is funny considering how long I've been blabbering on. I know that when I started telling this story, you probably thought it would be happy. Or maybe, you hoped it would be. Others, maybe, had a sense that it wouldn't be.

Jack was taken by the sea at around 10:25 am on January 30th. Gregor was taken as well, but the coast guard assumed that he was pulled into the drink permanently only a few minutes after Jack. All the while, the other guys in the boat where maydaying their heads off, but it was no use. None of them were capable enough to jump into that water to go after Jack and Gregor, and if they had, they'd probably suffer the same fate.

When I got the call, I was at my post, as usual, and I thought it was a crank call. I couldn't grasp what I was hearing, but the next thing I knew I was lying on the ground and there was an EMT team hauling me into a truck. I just blacked out.

When I awoke in the hospital later that night, I gotta tell you something, I wished to God that it was all a nightmare. I wanted it to be me out in that sea, drowning in the storm. I'd drown 1,000 times to have Jack back. I'd have my limbs torn off, all that shit.

There was no sense to it, of course. I had experienced that a lot in life when it came to tragedy. There was never any goddamn sense to it. Only the good ones were taken away, in my estimation. First it was Elizabeth, then it was Lily, and then my boy. My beautiful Jack.

Kids, I don't know why I'm telling you this. Hell, I don't even know why I'm calling you kids. It's just that, Jack's death will never make sense, and God only knows all the lives that were affected by it. But that night in the hospital, staring up at the blank television and considering ending my own life – if I may tell the truth – all I thought of was Annie. She had to have known by then. It was inevitable.

It was the first and only time since she arrived that I wished she'd never come to Newport. Not because she created any harm, but because of the harm that it had done to her.

I suppose that I'm not saying this right. Hell, I don't know what I'm saying. Forgive an old man.

There's nothing appropriate to say when it comes to grieving. No one can do it properly. It's the great mystery of life, and the great pain, and that's because it has no answers, no etiquette, and no rules. It's our animal existence. It's the great unknown. Never in my life did I think that it would happen to Jack. My Jack. One of the best, most honorable men I've ever met. And he was my son. My son. How goddamn lucky was I?

Chapter 24

In the days and weeks that followed, Annie didn't come into the SharkFin. She grieved in the way that she needed to. But later, she explained to me that all she could think to do for the first week was lie in bed and stare at her ceiling. There were profuse tears, of course, and she allowed those to fall copiously. June brought her food and asked Annie if the book club ladies could come over to support her, but Annie wanted privacy.

After a week of lying in bed, not eating a thing, Annie finally got up and took a shower. When she opened her front door, she was amazed by all the food that sat out there, and the flowers from June's shop. Thank God it was winter, 'cause otherwise, all that food would have spoiled.

She put the casseroles and containers of soup in the fridge – many of them frozen solid – and heated up a slice of banana bread that Myrtle had made from scratch. Annie took a couple bites of the bread and that was all that she could manage.

Annie explained to me that, in the second week, although she was on her feet, she merely sat in her chair by the window and looked out at the water. She could see Leavenworth from where she sat.

Her whole body was weakened from the endless weeping.

It's hard to explain how terrifying it is, to feel such bottomless grief. Waves of emotion came over Annie that seemed violent in nature, and then they'd run their course, and she'd go back to being a 'zombie,' as she called it. I know that she wanted to call me. She willed her fingers to pick up the phone, but it just wouldn't do.

The book was done but she couldn't bear to open her computer and look at it. In fact, she could hardly touch any sort of device. She had even forgotten how to use the coffee maker. I had to laugh when she told me about that one, but it makes perfect sense. The cloud of grief that one walks through, it changes the brain. It alters one's bearings in life. Annie dreaded stepping out of her apartment for fear that she forgot how to drive, or even walk down the street.

Now, I don't mean to disturb you with all this. Profound grief is something that all of us have trouble talking about. And you really don't know what it feels like till you experience it. But Annie got it bad. Real bad. Jack was the only good man to ever step into her life and love her unapologetically, and without need for anything in return. He just wanted to love her, similar to how I just wanted to love her.

Two weeks passed and Annie said she crawled into the third week, although there were faint glimmers of life. Rory left a voice message sending his condolences and apologizing for his conduct. Heck, I know that Rory was grieving, too. The whole town was. More food kept arriving at Annie's door, which she was grateful for, but there was one phone message in particular that seemed like it came from the Twilight Zone.

The bigwig from New York – the scumbag, as I like to call him – phoned Annie out of the blue, leaving a message. He asked her how she was and told her not to be a stranger. He didn't apologize for his conduct, of course. For disappearing when she needed him most. But that was all water under the bridge. Annie hadn't thought about him in quite some time.

Then there was the other call, and that one came from a chap called Nicholas at Sundance House, one of the fancy publishing houses in New York that Annie had sent her manuscript to, right before the storm. Apparently, Nicholas, a kid no older than a college grad, was excited about Annie's book and wished to talk with her about it. He wanted her to come to New York, or at the very least, have a video conference with the rest of the team at Sundance. In any other time, Annie would've been over-the-moon, but all she felt was faint amusement. She had a hard time grasping the meaning of it.

By week four, Annie got out of the house and was getting her bearings. At least she was able to accomplish simple things, like going to the store, showering every morning, and she even got in the habit of walking along the water, just to get her legs underneath her. I saw her one morning from a table at Barringer's Coffee, but she looked downcast and I didn't wish to disturb her. You may think that strange, considering all that Annie and I had been through, but something deep inside told me to give her space. She'd come to me when she needed me. And she sure did.

A gentle snow was falling outside on a Sunday morning. I'd just finished my standard breakfast of eggs, English muffin, and sausage, when I heard a gentle knock on the door of my shack. Pardon me for still calling it a shack, but it is what it is.

Anyways, I go over to see who it is, and when I open the door, I find Annie standing there, snow gently falling on her brown hair.

I stood there, frozen. "Annie."

"Can I come in, Tony?"

"Of course." I threw open the door and directed Annie to a comfy chair, but she wouldn't sit. We both just stood there. "Are you okay?"

Annie didn't reply with words, but merely ran into my arms and let me hold her. It was one of the most important embraces of my life.

"I loved him so much, Tony," Annie said through her tears, and I stroked the back of her head.

"I know, Annie. I did too. More than he knew."

"Oh, he knew." Annie pulled away so that she could look me in the eye. "And he loved you, too."

I hadn't cried in weeks, but I definitely let loose that morning. I poured Annie a cup of coffee, and we sat there the rest of the afternoon, talking about Jack and watching the snow fall.

In the months that followed, Annie slowly began to heal. A broken heart is a funny thing. There's no timeline for when it comes back together, but Annie was finding joy in the little things that she saw around her; the sight of the sun cascading across the water, the pleasure of a simple meal, the smiles on the faces of those she loved.

One morning in particular, Annie took a copy of her published book, *Surrender in Paris*, and brought it down by the water, clutching it to her chest. She considered the sea to be Jack's burial ground, and so when she received the first hardcopy of the book, Annie thought that it was fitting to share it with him first.

"Jack, look what I did." Annie spoke with childlike glee, tears streaming down her face. "I did it."

She imagined how Jack would've celebrated with her, the smile that would've been on his face, the way that he would hold her. In lieu of all that, Annie held herself, told herself how proud she was. It wasn't the same.

Boy, I wish you could've seen the book club when they celebrated Annie's triumph. Everyone had a copy, and they all cherished it. In fact, the first club meeting that Annie returned to, there wasn't a dry eye in the Newport Public Library. All the broads were in tears, not only for Annie's loss, but also for how much the book affected them.

June served champagne and Peggy had tried to make something out of a Julia Child's cookbook which turned into an utter disaster. June took secret satisfaction in that. They all couldn't believe that they had a successful author in their midst, and not only that, but Annie was in the process of writing her second book, which was going to take place in Denmark, of all places. Annie said that one day, when she was by the water, she thought of the famous mermaid in Copenhagen and an idea came to her. It was a love story, naturally, but perhaps that one wouldn't end so happily.

Newport Hollows was on the mend and June was a little stressed by how to run a B&B and a flower shop at the same

211

time. But business was good and so she hired extra staff to help out a bit. Samantha was going to be running the flower shop when she wasn't busy saving the world or advancing feminism. Gayle was also coming on as a cook at Newport Hollows. Everyone could trust a chubby cook. Sorry, I just had to say it.

As for me and the SharkFin, well, we were getting along okay. Spring was on the horizon and that was a damn good thing. Annie had been in a lot, which warmed my heart, but I didn't pour a drop of whiskey for her. There were many cups of chowder, plates of onion rings, and the occasional fish and chips. In light of everything, I was amazed by her appetite. I thought it was from the success of her book, but I would learn otherwise.

"I wish you served chowder in a bread bowl," Annie said one afternoon, sipping on a bubbly water.

"Hold your tongue."

"You're so elitist."

"The day the SharkFin serves chowder in a bread bowl is the day that I start drinking again." Annie laughed. "I'm not joking with you. It would drive me to drink, just to see it."

"Well, we don't want that to happen."

"Speaking of drinking." I looked down at Annie's bubbly water. "You've given up the sauce?" I couldn't help but ask.

"For the time being." Annie's face went pale.

"What is it?" I asked, seeing her expression change. She slowly looked up at me and her green eyes were sparkling. "What?"

"Tony, I'm pregnant."

The room started spinning. I didn't know whether to laugh, cry, or just jump out the window with excitement and disbelief.

"You serious?"

"Yeah, I'm serious."

"How long have you known?"

"About a month now."

I wanted to scream and say, 'You're just telling me this now?' But in light of everything that had happened, I can understand why Annie wanted to wait.

"Jesus Christ!" I cried, coming around the bar and guiding Annie with my hands from the barstool to a proper chair. I held her like she was a piece of rare glass.

"I'm not giving birth this moment, Tony."

"I know, I just thought maybe you needed to be more comfortable."

In hindsight, I was the first person that Annie told. I'm honored that she did so. And not only that, I was going to be a grandpa. Words can't properly describe the way that I felt when I heard the news. In a quiet, private moment, Annie would express to me her happiness, and also her fears. Fear that she couldn't provide the child with the home and family that it needed. Also fear that, in light of Jack's death, raising his child was going to be too hard, too scary.

The adventure that followed was a whole other story, my friends. Maybe I'll tell it to you sometime.

Chapter 25

Seven years after that day on the beach when Annie showed Jack her book and said her goodbyes, and here we stand today, back at the SharkFin, young Henry resting in his mother's arms. Henry has one of those smiles that lights up a room, and I hope that he always keeps it. I'll do everything in my power to make sure my grandson smiles as much as possible, and that he knows everything about his dad that there is to know.

"I want the soup," Henry says, playing with a napkin on the table.

"We can't do chowder right now, bug." Annie is holding him close and smelling his hair. "Grandma June is taking you to the diner for lasagna."

"Or we could just eat the pot pie," June jokes.

Henry gets excited. "Lasagna?"

"Yes, mommy has a little more writing to do. June is going to bring you home after lasagna and then we're going to read stories, okay?"

"Okay." Henry thinks that any situation that involves lasagna is A-okay.

"You get a lot done today?" June asks.

"Almost enough to make me satisfied."

Ever since Jack left us, a lot happened to Annie, and me. One thing that I do like is how frequently she comes into the SharkFin, but as I mentioned, it's always with the damn computer. She says it's because she has trouble writing alone. It makes her nervous. To this day, I don't know why.

"We gotta go." June stands up and puts out her arms. Henry climbs off of Annie's lap and jumps into June's arms, nestling his soft head into her massive bosom.

June's bosom isn't the only thing that grew over the years. Business at Newport Hollows is booming and she even had to expand the building to accommodate more guests. The flower shop is just the sweetest darn thing you've ever seen, and it became a popular tourist destination. June sells her chocolates there.

As for me, not much changed except for the fact that I just got older. And better looking, I'll have you know. Still living in my shack, and I'm happy with that. But nothing can fill the emptiness inside of me since Jack left.

Annie, however, is living at Leavenworth. Why is that, do you ask? 'Cause I own the place, and I wanted Annie and Henry to have it. It was a huge undertaking for her, but she had a lot of hired hands to help her with the massive property. The book club is no longer held at the Newport Pubic Library, but in Leavenworth's grand living room. The one looking over the water. Every New Year's, Annie goes out onto the balcony and thinks of their first kiss, then she wishes Jack a Happy New Year, holding a glass of champagne up high.

The Paris book was a huge success, followed by the thing in Denmark, which I hear was something of a colder love story. There were a few books after that. Honestly, I lost count. But the Tuscany book is the latest and the very thing that she is focused on at that table. As soon as June and Henry are gone, Annie dives back in with the precision of a surgeon.

I already offered the soup and she refused. To be honest, it's harder to get Annie to eat these days than it was when she first came to Newport. Of course, when she was pregnant with Henry, she ate like a pig. I miss those days.

I look over at Annie from behind the bar and wink at her. She smiles and turns her attention back to Tuscany. I don't mind so much that her head is always in far-off places, so long as her butt remains in Newport, if you know what I mean.

Sometimes, still today, when I look at her, I see that distraught girl with the crazy eyes, the mascara, the fear. One likes to think that a cozy town is a refuge of sorts from the outside world, but it isn't. The world still finds a way to come into your life, and it did for Annie.

Now, you're probably thinking I'm terribly morbid at this point, but that's not what this story is about. Heck, I shouldn't be telling you what this story is about. You can think for yourself. But I guess the point to all this is, sometimes folks come into your life that captivate you, fill you with happiness and joy. The only important thing, the only memorable thing about these silly lives of ours, is love. That's all that makes sense. Everything else is just crap. Pardon my language.

I look over at Annie one more time and she looks up at me. I mouth the words, 'I love you.' Annie blows me a kiss, and I'm happy as a clam.

CPSIA information can be obtained
at www.ICGtesting.com
Printed in the USA
LVHW082059180121
676819LV00005B/68